family

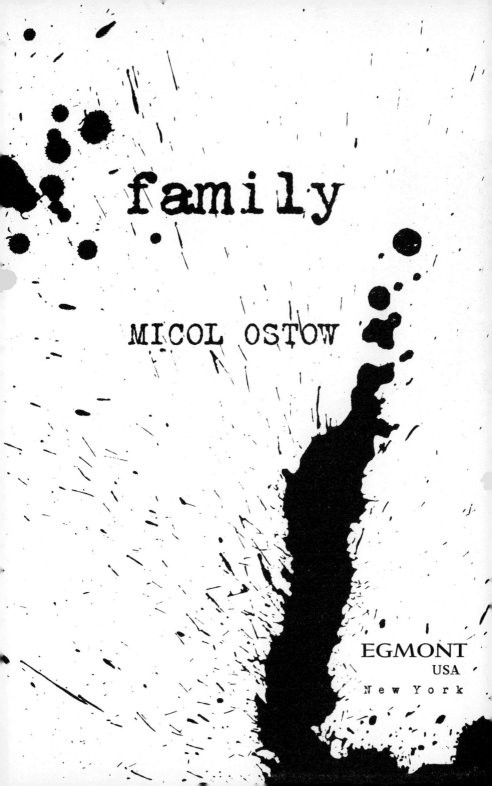

family

MICOL OSTOW

EGMONT
USA
New York

For Louise Hawes, my patron saint.

EGMONT
We bring stories to life

First published by Egmont USA, 2011
443 Park Avenue South, Suite 806
New York, NY 10016

Author's Note: *While I drew the inspiration for this novel from the Charles Manson family and the events of the summer of 1969, it is a work of fiction and not meant to represent any specific persons or time in history.*

1 3 5 7 9 8 6 4 2

www.egmontusa.com
www.micolostow.com

Library of Congress Cataloging-in-Publication Data
Ostow, Micol.
Family / Micol Ostow.
p. cm.
Summary: In the 1960s, seventeen-year-old Melinda leaves an abusive home for San Francisco, meets the charismatic Henry, and follows him to his desert commune where sex and drugs are free, but soon his "family" becomes violent against rich and powerful people and she is compelled to join in.
ISBN 978-1-60684-155-6 (hardcover) — ISBN 978-1-60684-197-6 (e-book)
[1. Cults—Fiction. 2. Communal living—Fiction. 3. Hippies—Fiction.
4. Abused women—Fiction. 5. Violence—Fiction. 6. Runaways—Fiction.
7. California—History—20th century—Fiction.] I. Title.
PZ7.O8475Fam 2011   [Fic]—dc22   2010043620

Printed in the United States of America

CPSIA tracking label information:
Printed in March 2011 at Berryville Graphics, Berryville, Virginia

"At my will,
I walk your streets
and am right out
there among you."

—CHARLES MANSON

part I

always

i have always been broken.

    this is something i've known forever, for at least as long as i can remember.

    it doesn't bother me anymore, this knowing, this fact that can't be danced around.

    the people who tell you that you can be put back together are wrong; they have their own ideas, their own agenda. i know this now. now, i know.

    i didn't, then.

    then, i would have died for someone to tell me that they saw in me a glimmer of hope, of wholeness, this idea that there was something about me worth saving, savoring, worth staying with. worth putting back together.

    i would have. *died.*

    and maybe it would have been better if i had.

    maybe. probably.

    this is something else that now, i know.

after

my hands are streaked with blood that is not my own.

my hands are streaked with blood, and there is screaming.

somewhere in the house, there is a high-pitched, constant screaming that has, by now, dissolved into the sort of ambient white noise that a person could tune out, easily enough, if she were so inclined. canned horror, like you might find on a sound-effects recording, or at a theme-park haunted house. so many voices. so much panic.

i am so inclined; i tune the shrill vibrato out, send it to a separate frequency, set it aside for the immediate future, as i tend to the issue of my stained, shaking hands.

how did they get this way?

i know the answer. i don't want to know the answer, but these are things i can't undo, can't un-know. things that are both my fault, my responsibility, as well as being beyond my control.

my hands shake, the blood pooling into the crevices of my gnawed-down cuticles.

"stay here, mel," shelly whispered, crouching in the door frame, her knife's blade glistening by a sliver of caught moonlight. "listen for sounds."

my hands shake. and even now, amidst the chaos, i am struck by how i have my mother's hands, though hers have never looked like this, would never look like this.

how strange to think that i should have my mother's hands. since i no longer have my mother, a mother, any mother.

i can't help but think that things could have been so different.

undertow

when i was twelve years old, i drowned.

luckily, it didn't take.

it was a family outing to the beach, the weather
cooperative, if "uncle" jack's temper

(not my father, never my father, i have no father),
less so.

i loved the beach. i still do.

i drowned, almost—

died, almost. really—

in a different, real way than how i'd drowned

(how i'd been *drowned)*

before.

but still, i loved the beach:

the ocean, the horizon.

i still do.

the water was cold, bracing, but once i'd eased in
past my shoulders, i hardly noticed.

instead, i focused on other sensations: the sting of
salt burrowing into the thin membrane of skin on my
lower leg, a slithery strand of seaweed brushing against
me. the movement of the ocean current against my
forearms as i paddled to tread water.

i felt strong, sturdy.

solid.

lightweight, too, which was slightly unexpected. it

had been so long since i'd been swimming; so long since i'd felt lightweight.

i bobbed along, tethered by the pedaling of my legs. i could still make out the shoreline, the figures projected there in silhouette, and i fixated, briefly, on a couple. they were young, but older than i was. they looked like they had stepped off the cover of a romance novel. he was chiseled, steely, all-american. she was soft, lush, sun-streaked. he lifted her, tossed her over his shoulder and pulled her into the surf as she pounded her dainty fists against his back in mock-protest.

i could hear her shrieks of laughter. i couldn't not-hear them.

i tilted back, recalled the game my mother and i once played together: looking for shapes in the clouds above.

there had been a time, now nearly forgotten, that my mother did play games, you see. eons earlier, ages long past. back before uncle jack came into our lives. she had managed to pass something along, after all. something other than the curve of her smooth, unlined hands. something that i struggled to recapture in that instant, alone.

it took a moment for my eyes to adjust against the burn of the sunshine behind the haze, but then i saw it: a face. bushy eyebrows, lashes, pupils, a speck of a nose, something you might see on a cartoon character. an upturned grin.

mother loved the unpredictability of cloud formations, the way that you could project onto them almost anything you wanted to see. it went against her need for either/or, her need to always know, one way or the other.

but that never bothered me. i liked to have a game with her, liked her reassurance that the images that flashed before me were in some unexplainable way, logical. that someone else could maybe see them, too.

except that she and i, we never saw the same images in the sky.

"a flamingo," she told me once, when i was much younger, jabbing a manicured finger upward. "the runaway bunny. a butterfly."

the streaks she pointed at expanded and collapsed under the imaginary weight of her fingertips, shifting. "a . . . ," she floundered.

i countered, my own hands stubby and unkempt, even then. she filed my fingernails for me; it was my own fault that i couldn't stop biting them. a vile habit, one i couldn't break.

"an evil wizard. the giant from 'jack and the beanstalk.' a sea witch."

i saw it, too, in the same clump of white that she'd been eyeing; her bunny's tufted ears were my giant's crooked fingers, beckoning.

it was a beautiful day, the kind that makes you feel that surely someone *must* have made a mistake, that there couldn't possibly be anything as perfect and whole as the earth, and yet.

yet.

even then, i saw it—a giant, with crooked, beckoning fingers. and i knew that even if he wasn't real, the version of our world being peddled on a sunny day like today was fleeting. that there *couldn't* possibly be anything as perfect and whole as all of that.

that there was something about a girl who insisted on seeing the ogre over the bunny. who *chose* that for herself.

i knew, even then.

even then, i was being pulled.

under.

back at the beach, motherless, however temporarily, a breeze tickled the tips of my shoulders, causing my skin to break out in gooseflesh. i shivered, and the tableau above reconfigured itself. eyebrows tilted in, pupils shrank down, mouth stretched to a thin line.

i shivered again. the shift was minuscule. a blink, a hiccup, imperceptible.

but swift. and unmistakable. the way that my mother could be.

back when i had a mother.

i bobbed along in the water, tilted myself. redirected my gaze from the shore to the horizon. it was endless. which made me want to follow it.

infinity has always felt impossible to me. there is nothing, after all, that doesn't end.

i had thought about it before, of course. about infinity. about shoulder blades and thighs, sturdy bodies and things that can and can't be shared. about mothers who don't mind if you go into the ocean by yourself, as long as you "don't go too deep."

about swift shifts, imperceptible but unmistakable.

i was shifting, drifting. i told myself that i was maybe being carried, that i wasn't actually making a choice.

but the truth was, *that* was a choice. that i *wanted* to drift, to be gone. to be weightless. it *was*. a choice.

so, there were pills.

colorful fistfuls, cascading through splayed fingertips.

but. it takes a lot of pills—a waterfall of pills—to become weightless, and halfway through, i changed my mind. just in case things didn't, actually, go on forever.

or just in case they did.

i told my mother. we pumped my stomach. didn't tell uncle jack, since he and his constant anger were off at work.

mother didn't bring it up again after that.

it seems to me that the type of people who see bunnies in the clouds are the ones who aren't going to nod in agreement when all you're seeing is a fairy-tale ogre who is looking to steal you away, to cause you harm.

which goes a long way toward explaining why mother and i so rarely found any common ground. how we—almost unwittingly, inadvertently—rubbed our tenuous connective tissue raw.

back when i had a mother, i mean.

there was a sharp whistle, and then hands. large, steady hands that slipped around my torso, clasping under my shoulders, firm, insistent. i inhaled sharply, looked up.

"i've got you."

another boy, also chiseled, steely, all-american. i flushed despite the chill of the water. "why?"

"you're a mile out." he nodded his head, gestured toward the shoreline. or, where i imagined the shoreline would be. i was shocked to find that i couldn't actually see it. i was a mile out. really.

"but . . ." this made no sense. i had only been floating.

"undertow."

of course. the undertow.

there had always been a pull directing me. *has* always been. pushing, stretching, applying pressure in every direction but home.

always.

i realize that now.

after

i listen for sounds.

they come to me, unbidden: a distant cricket, the rhythmic rush of a car passing along the road at the mouth of the canyon.

the hollow rattle of a rusted chain. a low growl.

something fierce, somewhere deep.

shelly. junior. leila.

others.

it takes a long time for a person to let go. sometimes.

i cover my ears. i shut my eyes.

the knife. i still see it.

and even with my hands pressed against my ears, i still hear the sounds.

something fierce, somewhere deep.

someplace inescapable.

Henry

if you haven't met Henry, it can be difficult to understand. everything, i mean. everything that came after finding Him.

or *Him* finding *me,* i should say. Henry was the one who came upon me, who rescued me, a grime-streaked skeleton perched, helpless. a heap of bones, a tangle of stringy hair, collapsed on a sticky park bench.

i was only angles and edges, featherweight, but lined with lead. that was how every part of me felt: heavy. immobile. rooted, however involuntarily.

but once you meet Henry, everything changes.

once you meet Him, you can't imagine a time or place where Henry doesn't exist, doesn't fill every inch of you, doesn't reach deep inside that bottomless pit where your soul used to hide and grab at your innards, pinch so forcefully that you can't help but to wake up, to realize: *now, yes.*

to realize: *this is what i have been waiting for.*

how it was:

i felt a shadow fall over my bare shoulder, felt His presence before i caught a glimpse of Him. He loped around the bench, smiled in such a way that the sky split open and washed over me, showering me with the certainty that this man held the secrets of the universe. and that He might be willing to share them with me.

i had secrets of my own, of course. Henry had guessed that just by looking at me. He knows things like that, like secrets sculpted of lead.

but universal understanding? knowledge? who could resist? i wanted everything that was promised in the landscape of Henry's face.

and, of course, there was His smile. always the smile, with its promise of the sky and blue and infinity and someplace other than sticky park benches.

Henry collects broken people.

i had thought it was so that He could fix them, could put them back together again.

now, i know different.

now, i know: it's not us that He is looking out for, in truth.

He has other reasons for gathering us, for knitting us together so tightly that we can't take a step, can't breathe without the next stitch—the next being, body—in our row. fusing us so tightly that alone, we would unravel.

He doesn't do it for our sakes. our family is not meant for us.

our family—*His* family—sustains Him. He feeds on us.

He does it to make Himself whole.

Henry's rules:

1. everything belongs to everyone. there are no parents, no ownership, no ego. no "i."
    2. there is no "why."
    3. there was no "before."

there is no i,
no why,
no ownership,
no ego,
no parents,
no before.

there is now.
there is always.
there is family.

and there is Henry.

now,
always,

Henry.

escape

it was easy to get away. easy enough.

getting away was the easy part. the struggle was in the decision.

or rather, knowing that the decision, the moment, had to come, was pressing against you with the force of your every molecule. knowing, but fearing, recoiling, shrinking still from that turning point, that fork in the road. that split-second, coin-toss choice.

never? now? or always?

and, really, *never* was the only viable option, the only possible solution, the only alternative, when you really, truly thought about it.

now meant "uncle" jack and whiskey breath and roaming hands and squeaking bedsprings.

it meant mother, treading water, understanding that jack was not your uncle, not your father, not your family. mother, watching you drown, doing nothing as you drifted, as the current pulled you to a place where whiskey breath and roaming hands couldn't reach.

mother, covering her ears, shutting her eyes.

mother, letting herself be steered by the undertow. leading by example. showing you.

always meant that i didn't have a choice. that there *was* no *i*. that everything—all of me—belonged to everyone. that uncle jack would forever be my uncle, that the undertow would forever carry my mother, that i would forever be pulled.

under.

tidal waves rushed at me, daily, nightly, filling my throat with salt water, gagging me until i couldn't say *yes*, anymore. but couldn't say *no*, still. couldn't speak. couldn't breathe. could only swallow, slip further.

so that the only way was to leave. to say: *never, now, always.*

so. i packed a bag—a backpack, really, more portable—with a few necessities. my two favorite tops, slender, spaghetti-strapped cotton pieces that hung from me loosely now that i was no longer so solid. i wore my lucky jeans, the ones that flared out over the beaded tips of my sandal straps, the ones so worn in the seat that i worried they'd split with one great lunge, one sudden move.

i tried never to make any. sudden moves, that is. i am not one for great lunges. sudden moves had never been my style. not until the *now, never, always* that was finally happening, i mean.

i braided my hair in one long tail down my back. i washed my face. i glanced in the mirror, droplets of water clinging to my eyebrows, the tip of my nose, my chin, like someone else's tears.

mel in the mirror didn't like being left behind, didn't like the idea of spending forever with mother and uncle jack. but mel in the mirror understood that i had to go. and that there were some things—so many things—that i couldn't take with me.

mel in the mirror knew that something important awaited me.

but she couldn't have guessed, really.

she couldn't have known about Henry.

gentle

the haight is like a broken promise, a premise that has gone unfulfilled.

i can't say for sure what it was that i had expected. maybe "gentle people," like the song suggests.

but even if the people in san francisco are gentle, i learn, even still—there are too many of them. too many bodies.

bodies. there are bodies everywhere.

tanned flesh, exposed skin, sinewy limbs. slitlike pupils and low-lidded eyes. bare, smooth, filed-down fingernails. soft, trailing tangles of hair.

torrents of skin and bone.

i didn't have a plan, really. just some worn dollar bills in my wallet, a backpack, and a grim determination to leave uncle jack, mother, and mirror-mel behind.

i had: a bus ticket.

i had: a vague, thin notion of the haight, and free love, and bodies, enveloping each other, welcoming, caring.

it wasn't much. i learned that quickly, with the first puff of fumes as the lumbering, barreling bus shuddered to a halt.

i didn't have: a place to stay. enough money to last me. food.

i didn't have: any of the things a body needs

to sustain itself, the things we all need to sustain ourselves.

the things that keep a body afloat.

the things that keep a body grounded.

right away, right after stepping down from the bus into a cloud of exhaust, i found my bench. sticky, stained, slats buckling slightly from age and moisture in the air, it beckoned to me.

i was tired, the sort of tired that creeps into your spine. i wanted to sit.

no, i wanted more than that:

i wanted some sort of infinity.

and suddenly, now that i had arrived, had made my way to my elsewhere?

now i wasn't sure that infinity was an option.

not here. not in the haight.

not the sort of infinity i'd had in mind, anyhow.

for two days, the bench became an island to me.

i did my best to plant roots there.

for two days, i was fixed, transfixed, swallowing, silently devouring, taking in the psychedelic endlessness that surrounded me: cloudless blue skies, muffled laughter, the languid movements of careless, gentle bodies in colorful costume.

and music. always music. the strum of a guitar, the echo of a bongo drum, the high-pitched lilt of a lullaby hummed half-silently.

at night i tucked my backpack underneath my
head, curled my legs together, and did my best to drift.
to stay afloat.

even when i closed my eyes, though, i was still
grounded. planted. rooted.

even when i closed my eyes, infinity still swam
past me, just beyond my grasp, brushing the tips of my
wriggling fingers.

carried by the undertow.

eluding me.

"here."

i started, startled, broken from my reverie.

i'd been doing nothing so much as staring into the
nowhere, barely absorbing, barely soaking in the images
that danced across my field of vision. there was music,
of course, and the heady smell of smoke that i now
knew opened all of the gentle people up, unfurled them,
carried them away.

"um. huh?" i rubbed at my eyes, pushed my lank,
dull hair behind my ears, and looked up.

< . . . >

focus.

interference flared behind the helmet of my skull.
white noise, the sort that pools at the back of your
throat the moment before fear sets in.

fear, or something sublime.

something fierce. somewhere deep. someplace
inescapable.

razor sharp, gleaming like a knife's edge.

a vortex, a black hole that began, ended, *everything,* with this.

now.

now:

a man.

older than i was, but still young. He wore faded jeans that looked soft to the touch—and i wanted to touch Him, right away, i wanted *so much* to touch Him—sandals, a gauzy white shirt, a leather vest. His hair was a deep chestnut, and it shone like the surface of the bay in the sunlight.

He had brown eyes like reflecting pools.

He looked kind, "gentle," as the song suggested. but it was more than that.

so much more.

He looked—how to put this?—He looked as though *He was looking.*

at me. *through* me. *into* me.

He was the undertow. He was the current.

He was the tide.

i sat up straighter, shuffled aside, and He smiled. gently.

seated Himself. gently.

"here."

i saw that He was holding something out: a cardboard cup, white, with watery blue writing on it,

like you'd buy from an outdoor vendor, from one of
the carts that is pushed in endless loops, meaningless
circles, hour after hour, just beyond the radius of my
weather-warped park bench.

"coffee."

i was *thirsty*, i realized. viciously, viscerally *thirsty*.

it was the kind of thirst that calls for clean, crisp
water. the kind of thirst that closes in on you, that
gums something thick and round like coffee in a lump
at the back of your throat. the kind of thirst that
chokes you.

coffee was not what i wanted. coffee would not
slake the thirst, dissolve the fists of sand collecting at
the base of my tongue.

but i couldn't decline.

i couldn't not-accept His offer.

i didn't want coffee.

but.

i wanted everything, anything, all of this man.
wanted to rub the threadbare gauze of His shirt against
my cheek, wanted to bury my dry, dusty fingertips in
the thicket of hair that gathered at the nape of His
neck. wanted to see myself, see the mirror-me!, to
luxuriate in how she might appear from within the
reflecting pools of His eyes, free of fault lines and fear. i
wanted to contemplate infinity from somewhere deep.

someplace inescapable.

i wanted everything, anything, all of this man.

i *wanted*.

i coughed, clearing out my insides, wondering what sorts of sounds would come out. it had been two full days since i'd uttered a word to another human being.

i said:

"th-thanks."

my voice sounded shaky to my own ears, a tire passing over gravel.

He didn't seem to mind.

i won't say that He didn't notice, because, of course, He did. even then, right from the start, it was clear that He noticed. He *noticed.* everything. but He didn't seem to mind about the stiff, broken sounds coming from within me. He smiled, passed me the water-blue cup.

i took what He offered me, sipped at the coffee gingerly. it was black, heavy, tart. it made my eyes water, filled my mouth with heat.

it burned.

i drank it all, downed the whole cup. first tentative, then growing greedier. and all the while, the man simply watched.

when i finished, i placed the empty cup on the ground. i suddenly felt self-conscious, suddenly had too many elbows, knees, strands of hair sticking to my cheeks like gossamer threads of a spider's web. i wanted to look to the ground, to look away, but i couldn't. i craned the open plane of my face toward the man like a crocus toward sunrise.

He laughed. "wakes you up, doesn't it?"

i nodded. He was right. i felt awake. awake like my half-life was a hurricane, a funnel of *never*, spiraling off into the distance.

awake like a crocus craning toward sunrise.

"i've noticed you," He said. He placed a palm on my shoulder, filled me with heat.

"i've seen. you've been here two days now, not a bite to eat, not another living person to talk to."

there was no reply. of course, i had no reply. of course, He was right.

He was right about it all, about everything, ever. and He had noticed *me*.

i had that sense about Him, overwhelming, enveloping, cloaking:

He. was. right.

He was inescapable.

"the haight. it's hollowed out," He said. "free love, all that? it's over, man. long over. it's well behind us. there are too many people here now, too many bodies."

He was right. He was exactly right. He knew about the bodies.

"did you hear about the 'death of the hippie'?"

i shook my head. of course i hadn't. i'd never heard about anything.

His eyes sparkled, then took on a faraway glint. He clasped my hand in His own, twined His fingers around mine, recited from a hymnal that only He possessed, a catechism that maybe He'd created Himself, words i hadn't heard before.

"it's a song," He said.

He said: "i like music. i like the way that it can bring forth a message. gently. y'know?"

His words were a poem. a prayer. a premise.

a promise.

well.

i didn't have a revolution of my own.

getting away had been the one thing, the only thing. and now what?

i didn't have a revolution to bring. and i didn't live anywhere.

so.

i didn't have an anything, an anywhere, an anybody.

i didn't know what was next.

infinity? maybe. for better or for worse.

"i have my own revolution," the man was saying.

i blinked, snapped back to attention.

"i have a place, my own place, with my own family. you'd like it." He was sure of this. "do you want to hear about it? maybe come see it for yourself?"

family. the word stiffened my spine, set like cement in my joints. mirror-mel called to me from behind her looking-glass prison, reminded me of how *family* ties could bind. could knot.

could fray.

family. hadn't i left that behind? hadn't i inhaled, held my breath, plunged headfirst into the undertow?

hadn't i drifted, open and expansive, toward the *now*?

something of mirror-mel's despair, her desperation, it must have seeped through. my flitting, fleeting panic exposed, i gave myself away.

the man surveyed me, taking stock. He read me like a topographical map, scanned the surfaces of my bare skin, studied my jagged fault lines.

seemed to come to a decision.

"it's not a family like what you've known," He said. His voice rushed with the quiet, assured force of a waterfall. "i can promise you that."

a promise. a premise. a pact.

about a new understanding of home. a haven. an afterlife.

His face split into a smile, poured like honey down the base of my throat, settled into the hollow where the blood pulses, where it presses up against the surface. blood, and fever, rushing with the force of a waterfall.

"how about this? you don't have to decide now."

relief, like a rainstorm. like an ice bath. it pooled between the soft webbing where my fingers met my palms, a force that i could almost touch. almost grab. grasp.

"we'll just take it slow, get to know each other."

family

the corners of His mouth stretched toward infinity. "my van is parked just off the road over there." He jerked a calloused thumb to demonstrate. "it would at least give you some shelter through the nights. while we get to know each other."

i shivered.

"would you like that?"

of course, i would.

of course, He knew that.

He was right.

always, completely, overwhelmingly *right*.

He was inescapable.

i nodded.

He grinned again, and a flash of flint flickered within me, glimmering from somewhere deep, from the black hole, from the vortex, filling me with the fever, warming me, spreading it from the outside in.

i wanted to drink Him in, to consume Him, to fold Him into my own body until we shared the same skin. i wanted to inhale Him until i overflowed. i wanted to be carried off, cradled, caressed. i wanted His infinity, His everything.

His undertow.

no matter, then, what *family* once was, back in the bottomless *before*. i *wanted*. still. yet. always.

i wanted to be His family.

i did.

He stood, dusted off His jeans, held His sturdy
hand out for a proper introduction.
"i'm Henry."

He.
was: Henry.
and i.
was: over, under,
locked in free fall.
spiraling into orbit.

smoke

i learn.

with Henry, i learn.

there are ways to silence mirror-mel, ways to
smoke her out. Henry knows; of course, He knows just
how to quiet her echoing sobs, to distill her razor-fine
muscle memory into a haze of vague interference. into
nothing more than the reverberation of a half-life.

Henry says there is no *before*. and He knows how to
bring me to the *now*.

He is magic, alchemy. chemistry.

soothing serum, an elixir.

He offers potions, medicines to break down inside
my body, invade my cells. my mind sparks and my limbs
loosen.

in His van, amidst the choked-off, heady
atmosphere, i swallow, i breathe, i take it all in,
welcoming. rushing toward the now. Henry's medicine
takes hold and the *want* slides over me, warm and
wiggling.

we take it slow.

first time

you couldn't call me a virgin.

not after all of those times with uncle jack, and whiskey breath, roaming hands, squeaking bedsprings. not after all of that endless struggling against the undertow.

but the first time with Henry felt different, still, somehow. it felt like the *real* first time, like the beginning.

of everything. of *always*.

it was like all that had come before had been merely practice. had happened to another someone. a cipher. a shadow. a mirror-image girl, covered in someone else's tears.

i didn't know that someone, not anymore. i wouldn't let her back. i swallowed her down and fought back the bitter aftertaste, ignored the chattering that rattled against the inside of my skull. i steeled myself against the constant ache of the fog, the vapor that i used to be.

if i didn't peer into the reflecting pool, i could pretend to will mirror-mel and her poisoned memories back, deep into the distance. i could build a dam, plug the channels leading to my former life.

with Henry, i didn't need a looking glass.

with Henry, i could define my own boundaries, my outlines, by the spotlights in his own unyielding eyes.

Henry saw me. saw *through* me, i mean. He heard the chatter as i ground my teeth together in tight denial of my bottomless past-life. my *before*.

He had his own ways to silence the white noise, the half-life, the mirror-girl.

the first night in the van, He told me. He showed me. He coaxed my tongue forward until it was outstretched: pink, soft, receptive.

He pressed the tab against it.

He stroked the underside of my chin as i closed my mouth, allowed the wisp of consciousness to melt away.

His eyes shone like marbles, like pavement after a rainstorm. He promised this would "bring me to *now*."

i wanted *now*, wanted Henry's *now* more than any other want. couldn't keep the want from running down the back of my throat, from seeping through the pores of my skin.

the van was big, bigger than two people really needed to be comfortable at night. we had sleeping bags, warm and downy despite the stuffing oozing from fraying corners and stains dotting the nylon surfaces. we rolled up our packs to use as pillows at night.

once the sun had set and the park had cleared of the respectable people, regular people, people like mother and uncle jack, Henry and i would stretch out in the back of the van.

Henry would play his guitar, or, sometimes, the

van's radio, the FM tuner set to rock or folk music, and He'd talk to me about His philosophies: that there was no such thing as ownership, that we'd all been ruined by our parents (clearly, i agreed), that the world was building to a fever pitch.

well. i didn't know about the world, had hardly even spent any time in it. but.

there was a fever raging. there *was*.

that much, i knew.

"let me be your father," Henry said, that first night, skimming the surface of my bare back with His fingertips. "think of me as your father.

"i can be your father."

Henry had dreams of becoming a musician, of hearing His own music wafting out from the FM tuner as He drifted off at night. He stroked my forearm as though strumming a guitar, humming to a melody that only He could hear.

i listened for sounds as he stroked. but there were things, even then, that Henry kept on the inside. tucked away. things quiet and imperceptible. things he hoarded, guarded close to the bone, in the hopes of making himself whole.

i didn't mind. i strained to listen.

i told Him i didn't have a father. and i couldn't think of Him, of Henry, as uncle jack, even if He was sort of behaving that way.

i couldn't. *never*.

because the difference between sex with Henry and
sex with uncle jack was that with Henry, i wanted it.
with Henry, i could never, ever get enough.

with Henry, i ignited like a supernova, lighting up
the atmosphere. it would be eras, eons, endlessness
before i broke the surface of the earth again.

three days. in the van. with Henry. with
consciousness. with swallows of smoke and hits
from tabs. with flesh, fingertips, devouring mouths,
drinking.

it was infinity. it was *always*.

"let me be your father."

"i don't have a father. i never had a father."

and hadn't wanted one. hadn't seen the point of
apron strings or family ties.

there was only ever binding. there was only ever
uncle jack. and the undertow.

"that's why."

"i don't want . . ."

i trailed off. it felt wrong, somehow, to disagree
with Henry, to go against Him. but there were things
i wanted from Him, things i wanted to do with Him,
things that a girl shouldn't do with her father.

i knew that. even broken, even *now*, *always*, *never*, i
knew that.

"you do. and i can. i can be your family."

family. the word no longer crumbled like sandstone.
now, instead, it swelled beneath me, carrying me
forward. rushing me toward *now*.

family.

He rolled on top of me, and the heat came flooding back. the fever.

"i can be everything."

after

junior cuts the telephone wire, steady, sure-handed.

leila clips the chains around the front gate, feather-weight, aflight.

shelly cackles, rubs at the greasepaint on her face. her eyes peer out at me, diamonds sunk deep within a pool of mud.

i follow them down the winding drive, eyes lowered and trained on the ground in front of me.

i listen for sounds.

and then i hear them:

gunshots.

i try to stop listening. to shut out the sounds. to quiet the fever.

but by now it is too late.

blood

leila may see through people, right to the core of their darkness. she was the one i watched out for, in the beginning. the one i always felt was watching *me*.

but shelly?

shelly has no mercy, no core at all. she is hollow. infinite.

shelly is the one who has actually tasted blood.

shelly is the one who craved it.

the ranch

it is like being in a movie.

the ranch is a sprawling, run-down, chaotic cardboard cutout, a facsimile of what real life is like for real people.

which suits me just fine. real life wasn't exactly working out for me, if you'll recall. real life never did me any favors.

Henry found out about this place, the ranch, through a friend. He has lots of friends, which works out well for Him. for Him, and for us, i am learning.

He tells me all about it, during our first three days in the van. i ask Henry about His family, His haven, and He explains about their homestead, the safe place where i'll be—*we'll* be—heading soon. the way Henry describes it, the ranch is love and openness and everyone caring. the ranch is family.

my family.

it used to be an actual film set, a wild, wild west backdrop. actors played dress-up here, make-believe—cowboys and indians and celluloid fantasy. there were shows you could watch on tv, in far-off houses where parents and children did such things as gather round nightly for wholesome entertainment. normal households, the types of households that none of us here at the ranch would know anything about.

Henry has told me, of course, about my new family. *our* family. a network of sisters and brothers, each of them shattered in some unique way, each of them— of *us*—searching for wholeness. each of us a patch, knitting together, in the hopes of keeping ourselves warm.

each of us unfurling, expectant. planting roots, transfixed, wet cement smoothed across the landscape of the ranch. setting. settling.

these days, the ranch is an outline, a suggestion of its former wholeness. no one films here anymore. truth is stranger than fiction these days. nobody is interested in the wild, wild west, what with everything that's going on today in the news.

not these days.

the new west has much more to offer people, in terms of fantasy.

that's where most of us girls on the ranch come from: the new west. or at least, that's where we met Henry. we were easy enough for Him to find, spotlights radiating out from behind the blank curtains of our eyes.

technically, i guess, we don't really come from anywhere. not anymore.

the west is a magnet, a beacon for broken people, and especially for us girls looking to escape from the infinite *before*.

so.

Henry collects us, His fantasies, and brings us back to the ranch.

to be together.
to be whole.
to be family.

arrival

the man who owns the ranch, emmett—
    the friend of Henry's friend's friend, *emmett*—
    he, *emmett,* is very, very old.
    he is a wisp of smoke, a death rattle, a suggestion
of *before.*
    i meet him on the day that i arrive.

    i am still stiff, blinking, sunlight-blind, fuzzy,
fizzing, from three days in the van with Henry. my
tongue is thick, my head buzzes with interference,
white noise. wind tickles against the pliant insides of
my thighs, the negative space where my jeans have been
rubbed through. the places where i am exposed.
    i have surrendered my photos, my driver's license,
what little money i had.
    the money was uncle jack's whiskey stash, and i'm
not sorry to have taken it. even if it is no longer my
own, mine alone, i am not sorry.
    everything belongs to everyone.
    he should be the sorry one, anyhow. uncle jack, i
mean. though i've learned well enough that waiting for
uncle jack to be sorry for anything is like waiting for
the mother ship to land, waiting for the moon to career
into the craggy canyons of death valley.
    waiting for *infinity.*

a girl, leila—one of my new *sisters*—takes it all from me: my bare, spare belongings, my everything, all that i surrender.

she grins at me, shows her sharp, slick canines. her cheekbones are cut glass.

my exposed places shudder and contract. Henry sees, palms the span of my head with His steady, sure hand, making my insides run like melted wax.

He beckons someone else toward us, a bright-faced girl whose cheeks bloom red.

he tells me her name: "shelly."

she swoons to hear Him call her out.

swoons to watch His lips curl around the familiar breath sounds, the awareness of her being.

Henry is the type that people swoon for.

shelly is the type to swoon.

"shelly," Henry says. "shel."

she gnaws at her lower lip, thrusts her pale fingertips into the front pockets of her cutoff jeans. eyes me with bemused curiosity.

if leila's face is a lockbox, shelly's is a blank journal, spine cracked, spread open on a worn tabletop. leila is a system of rapids; shelly is a life raft.

i cannot drown again. will not.

and shelly is a life raft.

she giggles. "you're new."

i pause, uncertain, and she reaches out. i want

to start, to shrink, but before i can collapse in, i am enveloped. shelly embraces me. her hair brushes against my cheek; i smell honeysuckle. the skin on her arms is cool, like a mother's against a fevered forehead.

she pulls back, holds me at arm's length. grins, giggles again.

"we're so glad you're here," she says, so calmly that there can be no room for doubt. *glad* spills out of her every pore, shines from the pupils of her sapphire eyes. her hand wraps around my forearm, squeezes and pulls me forward.

"you're going to love it.

"you're going to love our *family*."

sisters

shelly shows me around, introduces me to emmett.

she looks like leila, except behind the eyes.

i can see, as we walk the grounds, that all of us, the *sisters*, we all look somewhat alike. young, soft, clad in denim, cotton, leather sandals. fresh-faced.

open.

she's kinder than leila, too. shelly *is*. she is warmth. she is chatter and fire and laughter. she bubbles over with the thrill of revealing her wonderland to a newfound sister.

it has been eons since i've had a mother. ages since i knew a father.

and i have never had a sister.

before now.

i think about mirror-mel, wonder what people see behind *my* eyes. wonder if i would even recognize what lies there, myself. wonder if any traces of my dark shadow-self remain.

it strikes me: leila, shelly, and i:

we are, now, a paper chain, conjoined tracings.

infinite, ephemeral, inseparable.

now.

we are blood.

we are *family*.

fantasy

emmett's mostly blind, and can't hear too well, either.
shelly says he spends most of the day in a rocking
chair, on the front porch of the building he uses as his
home.

he lives in a whorehouse that is not a whorehouse,
above a saloon that is not a saloon.

even robbed of sight and sound, emmett still
shrouds himself in fantasy.

of course, robbed of sight and sound, fantasy may
be all that emmett has left.

leila keeps him company, keeps him happy. Henry
asked her to.

people do what Henry asks them to.

"Henry is jesus christ," shelly says to me.

we wind around the back of main street so that
she can show me the storage silos, the barns where we
will stay, the family. no movie sets for us. just love and
space and everyone.

Henry is jesus christ.

shelly says this very matter-of-factly, as though she
has just informed me that her favorite color is yellow, or
that her birthday falls in august. that my eyes are dirt-
brown. that emmett is blind, deaf, dying.

Henry is jesus christ.

she may be right.
maybe.

i smile, nod politely. shelly continues my tour of the ranch.

we turn, head up to the corral by the creek, where the children are kept during the daytime.

i wouldn't have expected children. had i come to this place with any expectations, that is.

"whose are they?" i ask.

they climb, crawl, coo, winding their way through the arms of sisters. young, open girls, girls who look just like me. paper-doll girls with blank, peaceful expressions.

conjoined, ephemeral. infinite.

inseparable.

i think: i would like to feel blank, to feel peaceful.

i think: Henry can make me feel that way.

i know: this is my *now*. and i am not sorry.

shelly shrugs. "everyone's. they're everyone's children. we raise them together."

everyone.

i realize: we are all, here, *sisters*, *mothers*, *daughters*. all of us is everyone.

now.

yes.

family.

shelly explains that emmett lets us stay because
he likes the company, likes to have pretty girls around
cooking for him, even if he can't quite make out their
delicate features with his ruined eyes. likes to have
young men—boys, really—tending to the maintenance,
keeping the ranch from sinking further, sliding into
total disrepair.

keeping the death rattle at bay.

we are here to sustain the fantasy. we are *all* here to
sustain the fantasy.

emmett's.

Henry's.

possibly, our own.

real life wasn't exactly working out for us. for *any*
of us, i realize. real life never did any of us any favors.

"and?" she adds, "i think he mainly likes leila."

that makes sense.

i'm not sure how i feel about leila yet, myself. but
still, it makes sense. leila is the opposite of death; she is
a live wire, coiled, potent. maybe poisonous. how could
emmett be immune?

"it's the perfect place for us, for our family," she
goes on.

at first i think she means the ranch, the corral, the
barn. i think she means how lucky it was that Henry
came upon it, even though with Henry, of course, it's
never luck. it's all His doing, it's all His will, His way.

then it dawns on me, like a cloud of realization. like

one of Henry's pills, like his cache of magic smoke, like a tab of enlightenment melting on my tongue:

she means Henry. the half-life of Henry.

His orbit is the perfect place for our shrieking, shrinking, fractured souls.

she may not know she means it, but she does. i see it as sharply as emmett must see leila's black-widow webbing.

"lots of room here for anyone who wants to come and share in Henry's love."

her eyes sparkle. she overflows with Henry's love. she is *bursting* with it.

and something else. something i can't quite put my finger on.

something i maybe don't *want* to think about.

shelly is my sister. and that is enough. for now.

more than enough.

for now.

that is *everything*.

"if we can keep it under control, fly under the radar? we could stay here forever."

the lilt to shelly's voice tells me she would like this, that *forever* is what she yearns for.

i have to wonder, even just for a moment, what sorts of things need to be kept under control.

no matter; i am well versed in the fine art of flying under the radar.

i should fit in well here, soaking in the syrup-
strong glory of Henry's love. in the orbit of His half-life.

i could overflow here, burst. with love. and maybe
something else.

shelly is wrong, though. about Henry being jesus
christ.

i don't tell her as much—those sparkling, *forever-*
eyes worry me in some secret corner i choose to
shy away from—but i'm sure of it in my soul. it's an
inescapable fact, like two plus two being four, or me
having dirt-brown eyes, or uncle jack and his drinking:

Henry *can't* be jesus.
jesus never did anything for me.

i don't believe in jesus christ.
only in Henry.

leila

i only had twenty-one dollars on me when i arrived at the ranch, lucky jeans having finally given out, a thin layer of dust coating one of my two favorite tops, the straps of my sandals loosening from their scuffed foot beds.

it was enough for leila.

she smiled at me. it was a different smile than the one Henry had flashed when He came upon me at the park bench, like the messiah ready to show me to the gates of ever after.

leila's smile was closed and mysterious, like she'd read your diary or visited you in your dreams at night. like she knew your dirty secrets.

like she knew how best to make you bleed.

"i'll need your wallet." her lips parted. she wore her hair like mine, in a braid, but hers was tighter, her eyebrows creeping steadily toward her scalp.

i blinked, disoriented from the three-day trip spent in Henry's van. leila's face was expressionless, save for the parted lips. at first i didn't realize that this was how she smiled. how she said hello.

how she asserted herself.

"go easy on a new sister," Henry said.

even with His easy tone, it wasn't a suggestion. with Henry, it was never a suggestion. never anything less than gospel.

"i'll need your wallet." leila didn't flinch. i guessed that she was my age, but older. somehow.

there was a hidden language, a code shared between leila and Henry. i was jealous. i'd stumbled upon a lost world, an ancient language, and i'd misplaced my guidebook. their eyes were a sealed fort, unified. i was weaponless, guileless. adrift as ever.

i gave her my wallet.

"i don't have much cash," i said, handing the lump of weather-beaten leather to her.

she nodded, not looking at me, flipping the wallet open. she glanced at my ID: a driver's license showing a snapshot of another girl, a mel from the before.

"melinda jensen. seventeen years old."

i thought again:

she, leila—

she is my age. but older, somehow.

i shrugged. "that's me." i peered at the picture upside down in her smooth, pale palm.

even then, there had been cracks behind my eyes. a camera couldn't hide those sorts of fissures, rivulets, fault lines. i could see them, now, from where i stood. Henry had seen them. leila could see them. they were permanent.

leila slipped the license out of the wallet, quickly dropping it into a tin box with a lock on the front, like a tool kit, or a tackle box. the box was heavy, permanent; something solid, sturdy enough to house the ghost of my former self.

something to capture and contain the hairline fractures of my past life. my half-life.

she wasn't finished. she continued to riffle through the wallet, examining the contents. her fingers paused, danced against a thick square. photo paper.

like a magician coming to the end of a trick, she offered her palm to me again; from its center, half-life mel winked out, flanked by mother and uncle jack. the unholy trinity.

"cute," she said. she deftly deposited the picture in the lockbox, letting it float until it settled, covering my driver's license.

"i might have wanted that," i said.

leila didn't seem to care what i might have ever wanted. she leveled me, eyes storm-gray. she snapped the box shut and jiggled its combination, sealing its contents. severing my ties. cutting me off from my former self.

i *didn't* want the picture. i didn't need the license. wouldn't need either, here at the ranch. not the money, either—Henry said that the family took care of each other. leila knew this, knew *me*, in an instant.

leila was my family, now. leila and i were bound. leila was blood.

"it'll be here," she said coolly.

"everything stays here."

dolls

i wanted a barbie.

when i was seven years old, i wanted a barbie doll for christmas.

i didn't care which one—and there were so, so many: a doll for every fantasy, for every possible escape, for every alternative to real life. your barbie could be a nurse. she could drive a car (pink, and convertible, obviously, the better to offset her painted complexion, ideal for allowing the breeze to tousle the stiff, synthetic strands of her candy-floss, gold-spun hair). she could carry a briefcase, or a hatbox. she could sing in a cabaret, dance in a chorus line, ride in a rodeo.

barbie could do anything but wear flat-heeled shoes.

anything but speak, or move on her own. those were not prerequisites for the complete, full-flourish, barbie experience.

or so i imagined.

thus far, barbie was only a fantasy to me. a pastime for other girls. girls with real fathers, mothers, *families*. girls with gold-spun hair.

girls i'd never known. would never be.

i wanted a barbie for christmas.

but. christmas with mother and uncle jack was a time for disappointment.

i knew instantly that year, upon seeing my present under the tree, that it wouldn't be a barbie. the box was too big, lumpish, unevenly wrapped, even for one of her endless accessories. barbie accessories are packaged smooth and slick, ripe for pristine presentation. so. it couldn't be.

in a way, it was better to know like that: all at once, no time for false hope to marinate, to work its way under my fingernails and behind my ears before finally taking hold of the space inside my rib cage. the space i mostly kept tucked away, quiet, ironclad. it was better not to expect. better not to forget the true meaning of the constant hum, the tacit pressure of endless *almost*.

better to know—swiftly, simply—what real life tended to hold in store.

i feigned enthusiasm (jack was always a stickler for enthusiasm, however false) and pulled at the wrapping. paper; ribbon; glossy, sticky tape gave way to a monstrosity:

a life-size baby doll, birthed into my bewildered arms.

"you can feed her. and change her diapers." mother seemed pleased at the prospect.

i was baffled. not surprised, exactly, never quite surprised; i knew too much for surprise. had never let hope take hold. but feeding and changing a baby doll? my own mother had never shied away from sharing with me the idea that motherhood hadn't been her first choice, but rather, a last resort.

my own mother hadn't wanted a baby. hadn't wanted *me*.

my own mother's fantasy, from what i understood of it, even then, was about as far away from motherhood as a person could possibly get. why, then, would she ever think that make-believe motherhood was a gift to be passed along?

christmas was a time for disappointments. and motherhood—make-believe or otherwise—was, perhaps, the biggest disappointment of them all. we were keeping on theme, at least.

i ignored my gift. crafted crude paper dolls from thick, dull construction paper instead. sketched outfits for them that were better suited for a pool party at the barbie dream house than christmas dinner in anywheresville.

i thought about fantasy: my own, my mother's.

i discovered something else my mother had managed to pass along to me, after all:

the void, the vortex. the endless, empty chasm of never being satisfied.

her orbit was a black hole; she was antimatter. we couldn't fill each other up, mother and i, couldn't even fill ourselves up.

but i couldn't bring myself to completely let go, either.

not that it did me much good.

i was skating, scraping at the edges of the confines

of my life, fingers curled, toes flexed like the soles of a
plastic plaything.

    i was clinging.

    while mother pulled endlessly further away.

campfire

Henry had told me about the campfires that He would hold at night, but it was different, being there.

being there was quiet. holy.

more, even, than what i imagined, those three days there in the van. i couldn't have imagined this much.

being there made me feel special, like a magnet tugged at all of the tiny ions in my body and tilted me toward Henry. and in that, i was connected to every other jagged shard that He had collected. connected to every member of our sea-glass circle of *family*.

the fire threw off heat, baking the edges of our skin, drying our eyes, and coaxing our own fever outward. warming us at our collective core.

on my first night at the ranch, i don't have to cook.

on my first night, i am treated like a guest, like a princess, like a treasured object.

i meet my sisters, and though i can't yet recall each of their individual names, i know it is no matter. they understand. they feel my love, my wells of gratitude. and in response, their faces radiate light, protection, welcome.

i am a part of this group, instantly. folded in, enveloped.

i meet brothers, too. some brothers, a few. young boys with blooming cheeks and hair almost as long as my own. they wink and chuckle, appear pleased to meet me. happy to know me. to have me.

they *are*. the brothers.

they are here, shelly explains, to help Henry. to aid emmett. to assist with all of the infinite endlessness of life at the ranch.

"there are some things you need a boy for," shelly says. the corners of her mouth turn up as she responds to the punch line of a joke i haven't yet been let in on.

i nod as though i understand. as though i get it.

here, now, i want to get it.

i want to hold it, to have it all. to claw my way up the dank, slippery walls of my ink-black well and find my way to this bright, enlightened, newborn family forever.

i nod as though i understand. as though i get it.

and i know that soon enough, i will.

after shelly finishes my tour, and the sun begins to set, the rest of the girls set about fixing dinner for the group.

"we take turns," shelly explains, though she obviously isn't taking a turn tonight, and she doesn't offer as to when her turn generally falls.

i suppose they have a system worked out.

they—this family—have worked it all out. and they work together. they *all work*. together.

the ones who are cooking don't seem to miss her, don't seem to mind; they move smoothly, their preparations a choreography that they've each committed to heart.

pots rattle and drawers clang and from somewhere, someplace that has somehow until now escaped my curiosity, several mangy dogs approach, sniffing eagerly, but managing not to be underfoot.

they, too, understand the system.

the rhythm here is metered, measured, tuned to a frequency that even the animals are aware of.

Henry's influence, His orbit—it's what does this. it's what binds these people. it's the opposite of my mother's half-life, the black hole that nearly crushed me, pulverized my stony places into a fine dust of *no, not now.*

never.

Henry's half-life fuses, fixes, folds people inward. where my mother's only ever pushed me away.

when dinner is ready, Henry gathers us around the campfire, a leaping, dancing bonfire out behind the barn. it is just as He described it to me when we were off in the van on our own: pixilated stars piercing the inky depths of the sky, girls and boys with scrubbed faces and long, flowing hair, crouched, happy, eating to their fill.

there is one hitch that i learn quickly, though.

bowls are passed out, and spoons. i peer into mine: some sort of soup, or stew. it smells of garlic and smoke, but even if it smelled like nothing but clear blue air, it's fine; after three days of service-station snack food, i could eat just about anything. i dip my spoon into the bowl.

immediately, there is a sharp elbow poking into my ribs. shelly's elbow.

i turn, confused.

she points to a spot just to the left of the campfire, to where the dogs have reappeared, eagerly devouring bowls of food of their own.

"we have to wait until they're finished," she says.

it takes me a moment, as she jerks her head, until i get what she means:

they.

as in: the dogs.

we have to wait until the dogs are finished.

i glance at Henry, and at His side, junior, the tall cowboy type with the toothpaste smile. shelly told me earlier that he tends to emmett's cattle.

right now, junior is eating. *scarfing*, in fact: scooping mounds of soup from his bowl and shoveling it straight into his mouth without even swallowing. a thin dribble of liquid runs down his chin, snaking an oily, pungent trail through the early-evening scruff of his sculpted jaw.

junior is not waiting. for anyone or anything.

"the *girls*," shelly says, seeing the puzzlement on my face. "the girls have to wait."

i glance around the circle and see that she is right; none of the girls are eating yet. several bounce babies

from the corral on their laps; most are content to
simply stare off into space. leila is stretched back on her
elbows, the sleeves of her peasant blouse pushed up,
sandals kicked off and bare feet pointed toward the fire.
she wiggles her toes, sighs.

her face has relaxed, and i realize that though her
features are sharp, cruel, she is pretty.

all of Henry's girls are pretty.

does this mean *i* am pretty?

Henry finishes with His food, sets His bowl beside
Him, grins. flames flicker, framing His face. His cheeks
are tinged with a deep orange glow.

"aren't you hungry, mel?" He asks.

i get it: this is how He tells me that it is time. for
me, for the girls to feed. this is how He tells us.

i get it.

"aren't you hungry?"

and i am.

i *am* hungry.

more than that, even.

i am *starving.*

Henry indicates that it is time for me to eat. for
me, and all of my sisters.

so i do.

we all do.

later, shelly explains it.

"it's a sign of respect," she says, "that the girls eat last.

"it's a sign of His respect."

last but not least, i think.
or even: *saving the best for last.*

it's a sign of respect. *Henry's* respect.
i can see in shelly's eyes how much she wants me to understand, to *get it,* like the punch line from that near-forgotten joke.
her *want* is enough for me.
more than enough. it's everything.
and. well.
after all: *respect.*
of course.
no wonder i didn't recognize it.

music

after we have all eaten our fill, Henry takes out His guitar.

when Henry plays guitar, it is easy to see how shelly could mistake Him for jesus.

myself, i suddenly wonder if in fact i do believe in god. (i have no doubt about how it is that i believe in Henry.)

i know it's a cliché to say so, but Henry plays guitar like an angel.

assuming that angels can play guitars.

i figure that angels can do whatever they want to do. just like Henry. and anyway, it's not angels i am interested in right now.

He plays folk music, the same music He played for me in the van, and it's clear that all of the people here, all of His family, know His music well.

they sing along, hum, bob their heads, sway. they wrap their arms around each other, form tight cocoons. they touch, stroke, smile. the babies have long been put to sleep.

"He's going to be famous," shelly says to me. and i believe her. "He's going to spread our family's music. and love."

seeing everyone, all of Henry's *family,* swaying in tune, in concert, together, i believe her. i believe *it.*

family

63

junior brings out a pipe, the tall, smooth, blown-glass type that i'd seen in storefronts when i first arrived in san francisco. Henry passes him a small plastic bag filled with something thick and green.

i know what that is, inside the bag. Henry and i smoked some while we were in the van. it's different than the tabs He gave me; more mellow, less severe.

but in the end, they are the same. in the end, they are *all* the same, really: they are all something to carry you away. a chemical undertow.

after the pipe has been passed from outstretched palm to outstretched palm, Henry sets aside the guitar. He winks at shelly, who wanders over to junior's side of the circle. she leans down to him, rubs his shoulders for a moment, pulls him up, and the two of them stumble off toward the barn.

leila giggles and rolls her eyes. she has hitched her shirt up like she's sunbathing, and i can see the flat expanse of her stomach.

Henry catches her eye and laughs with her.

"dirty hippies," He says. meaning shelly and junior, who are off to fuse their fevers, to collide their tides, to consume each other oh-so-casually.

this is what family does.

it is what family—even *Henry's* family—does.

even. still. of course. *always*.

some things, so many things, are *always*.

i pause, reflect, and find that i am not surprised.

this family is flowing—*overflowing*—with love. this

is how we share it with each other. how we collect the
runoff as it spills down the surfaces of our skin. we are a
chain of paper dolls, connected.

Henry catches my eye across the bonfire, asks me
an unspoken question.

He knows, of course—knows my reply before i
even have the chance to cock an eyebrow, to twitch a lip.
He sees me. sees *through* me.

He knows that i am not surprised.

in the haze of smoke and tide and undertow, i
understand. i *get it*.

i see—how it is that this family works. how we
share. collide. fuse.

burn.

i am lightweight. i am afloat.

at peace. ready.

to love and be loved.

with my family.

dirty hippies. that is what they are—what *we* are.

Henry is joking, of course. Henry knows there is
nothing dirty about our family's love. but. it's what
uncle jack would call us. and *he* wouldn't be joking.

when uncle jack would read about the new west in
the paper—about the drugs and the sex and the boys
with hair almost down their back—disappointment,
disgust, would drip from his voice.

"dirty hippies. diseased, you know. all of that free love.*"

free love.

i couldn't say for certain what was going on with shelly and junior back at the barn. i mean, i had an idea, of course. something about music, and *now*, and tidal shifts. but.

"free love"?

i still wasn't sure.

to me, that kind of love, the sex kind, didn't ever really come free. that kind, the kind among family?

that kind, i learned from uncle jack, always had a price.

it was uncle jack's love that was diseased, uncle jack's love that changed the way i felt about love in general—any kind of love, all love.

the only free love was Henry's.

and i was sure of only one thing, in that moment:

i was going to take what i could get of it. for as long as i possibly could.

hooking

when Henry found her, shelly tells me, she was—*where else?*—in the haight, hooking.

"well, technically," she says, "topless dancing. but it was never enough money, and there were always men willing to pay for something extra."

in the parking lot outside of the strip club. that's where the "extra" would happen, where she turned her tricks. except, she doesn't call it a strip club. she calls it an *exotic nightclub.*

whiskey breath and roving hands: how exotic.

shelly is originally from oregon, she says. like me, she never had a mother. and her father showed his love the same way uncle jack did. shelly knew disease and fever.

like me.

"so frankly," she says, "stripping seemed like a big step up. at least i was getting paid."

shelly was one step ahead of me. she knew, even then, that there was no such thing, really, as "free love."

she is not self-conscious, either; unlike me, she will happily shed her clothes as a snake shakes off its too-tight skin, will gleefully wind her way around the campfire at night, bathing in flames and warmth and light and Henry's orbit. she thinks nothing of offering her body, welcomes the touch of someone, anyone, the family, reaching out to share her, cup her, coax her, hold her. drink her in.

Henry helped her, she explains. to remove her doubt, her second thoughts, her mirror-self. to let go of the half-life and shake off her too-tight skin. she has been reborn.

through Henry, she has been reborn.

let me be your father.

it sounds familiar; i should be jealous, could very easily be jealous. but of course, there is more than enough of Henry to go around. enough for everyone, for our entire family.

Henry is infinite.

i learn the story of how shelly met Henry at a party: one of the other dancers from the *exotic nightclub* was having people over, and of course, shelly was in. shelly was always in, always up, always down for anything: free drugs, alcohol, drinking in skin. anything to beckon the undertow back, to help to fold it, slide it beneath the surface again.

"He walked in," she tells me. "Henry. and the entire room just—*whoosh*—dropped away."

she waves her hand to show me *whoosh*. she doesn't have to. i know that feeling, the spinning, yawning, antimatter sensation that comes from Henry's orbit.

"i knew right then that there was something special about Him, that He was someone i was supposed to meet. supposed to be with."

she sighs.

He was with another girl that night, someone He'd
brought with Him to the party. not leila, but one of the
others, someone named margie, or merri, someone who
hadn't stuck around. He had invited shelly to come stay
with them in their apartment—back then, He'd had an
apartment (how conventional, ordinary, everyday, how
jarringly *normal*)—which shelly did. but it turned out
margie-merri wasn't one for sharing.

unlike shelly, margie-merri wasn't in, up, down for
anything.

margie-merri—and here shelly snorts and rolls
her eyes—she didn't understand that Henry was too
much, so much, filled to bursting. that He couldn't be
contained. that it would be selfish not to share Him.

margie-merri would rather have forsaken all Henry
than sacrifice her own small bit, the amount of Him
that she could fight in one tightly balled fist.

i think: it is just as well that she didn't stay. i would
never have understood her, margie-merri. i could never
get someone like that.

clearly, margie-merri had no sense of family.

and there is no room for that sort of thinking, here
on the ranch.

here, now, *forever*. on the ranch.

obviously the little apartment in the haight wasn't
big enough to hold Henry and all He had to share. it

wasn't long before He bought a van secondhand and headed out to the desert, out to the ranch, out to *forever*, family in tow.

it was dreamlike, this idea, this notion that we had all just up and followed Him. like something out of a fairy tale, out of a storybook. out of a fable scripted in a dead language, scratched on wafer-thin parchment in spindly scrawl etched in disappearing ink.

but did that make Henry the pied piper? or the golden goose?

it made a difference, you see:
whether we'd clutched at His tail feathers in the hopes of brushing our fingers against something gilded.
or whether we were infested, *we* were the vermin, and He, Henry, was leading us out, away, gone.
dirty hippies. free love.
it made a difference.
but i couldn't be sure. not then.
not yet.

junior

junior wants.

    according to shelly, back in his old life, back in the *before*, junior was some kind of small-town god.

    attractive, amiable, athletic. a classic american good-old-boy hero.

    on the surface, junior is the most wholeness i have ever encountered. even teeth and sandy hair and eyes like ocean. eyes like *infinite*.

    still, though: he is here. in the *now*. in the fractured fantasy.

    he is here; therefore, he is broken. *must* be broken.

    it is an unavoidable piece of logic: in his own way, junior is fractured, shattered, shrinking. running out his half-life just like all the rest of us, here on the ranch.

    i see the way he seeks approval. takes it as the mark of confidence that it is when Henry awards him a girl, two girls, a group, a gaggle, for the night. these things make junior feel important, which Henry understands.

    Henry understands: junior *needs* to feel important. Henry can do that for him, and does.

    Henry knows how to give people what they need.

    my first night here, my first campfire. Henry picked. *me*.

shelly and junior wandered off, entwined.

and Henry rose.

"dirty hippies."

He winked. it was the punch line to a joke, but finally—i *got* it. i understood.

we: all of us. all of our *family*. we'd been made to feel dirty, outside, other.

but this, the ranch: it was, is, always will be home.

here, we have nothing to explain, nothing to account for. here, we are only ourselves.

and we have one way—our own way—to fill our hollow places up.

free love

the fire throws sparks.

    i stretch forward, unafraid. i like to feel the flames lap against my cheeks.

    "mel," Henry says, His voice like a clap of thunder, "will you come with me?"

    no one has ever asked before.
    certainly not uncle jack. never.
    so when Henry takes me to the barn, to shelly and junior and hunger and hands, i go with Him.
    i go with Him. i go slack. i give myself over.
    and when shelly puts her mouth on mine, puts her hands on me?
    with Henry watching, His gaze sharp, potent, approving?
    i follow her mouth, her hands, with my own. i fill her hollow places.
    i float.

ice

with junior, though, it is different.

junior's hands are cold. just the tips of his fingers skating along my bare skin makes me shudder, makes me shrink.

makes me fold in on myself.

with junior it is different.

i know, though, what Henry expects of me. and so i go along. He has been so much, so many things, for me, given so much *to* me. i cannot disappoint Him.

and so. i tune myself to another frequency. i detach.

but i cannot float. not fully.

junior is too cold for that.

through my squeezed-shut eyes, i can still see junior, so clearly. i see him like he is carved of glass, ice, crystal. my eyes go right through him, and i am relieved when he collapses, finished. pulls away from me.

shelly puts a hand over mine. Henry drapes an arm around my shoulder, kisses me on the forehead like i imagine a father would.

i can be your father.

"i told you," He says.

"i told you that you would love my family."

i nod. His voice is a lullaby, and i begin to sway, to give myself over to the haze and the clouds and the undertow. the ogre in the sky is breaking apart, reassembling himself into a cocoon of safety. that is the power of Henry's orbit. His pull.

His half-life.

still, though: i see.

i see junior. see the way that junior *wants*.

i see the way he soaks in Henry's aura, basks in Henry's light.

i see the way that he embraces the fever.

he is glass, ice, crystal.

and he is primed to shatter, to splinter.

to melt.

after

the man on the sofa shakes his head, pushes himself up on one elbow. sleep crusts the corners of his eyes.

he blinks, shakes his free wrist, peers at his watch. his hair is flattened, pressed against his skull from where he dozed off on the sofa.

he looks small, disoriented. confused.

"what time is it?" he asks. "was i—?"

then he takes in junior: six feet tall, clad in shadow, cheek spattered with mud.

junior, bearing down on him.

"who are you?" the man on the sofa asks. he is still uncertain. still not quite concerned, not too terribly worried about the turn that this evening has taken.

he should be.

junior draws himself farther, higher, until he is tall as a tree, a tower, a tornado.

he slides his pistol from his waistband, cocks it.

click.

my stomach clenches, a swarm of hornets, fluttering wings locked in beat.

"i'm the devil," junior says.

"and i'm here to do the devil's business."

then: silence.
then: sounds.
then: fever.

and i can do nothing to stop it. not any of it.
the half-life, the orbit, the vortex has opened, and
we are all being pulled inward.
we are all being crushed by gravity, by antimatter,
by the yawning black hole.
we are all collapsing in upon ourselves.

trash

"you wouldn't believe the sorts of things that some people throw away."

this is what shelly says to me.

she tells me about the things that people, most people—many, many more than you might think—cast aside.

she explains that people are wasteful, careless, empty. human beings *are*. that they have no sense of the value of objects.

human beings waste all kinds of things.

specifically, human beings waste food.

and this is how the family, our family, *Henry's* family, has learned to eat. has discovered the way to feed ourselves.

we eat what other people toss, what they reject. what other human beings waste.

and. we eat *well*. it is almost too much to believe, but we do. we eat *well*.

it's part of the system, part of the process, this hunter-gatherer method that the girls have, at Henry's suggestion, devised.

once a week or so, a group of us, maybe two or three, are sent to the nearest town—about fifty miles away, at least an hour by car—where we park behind local restaurants.

"and you just . . . *beg*?"

i cannot fathom this, can't imagine the outstretched palm, the plaintive face. the bald need, the raw, open request.

never mind what might have happened if i hadn't been found, hadn't been adopted, been *collected* by Henry on the park bench, that day, in the haight. never mind that *i* might very well have been reduced to begging to fill my porous membrane.

to plug the holes, to fill the *wants*, the needs.

i *might* very well have been. but He did. and so i wasn't.

i wasn't. because of Henry.

which means: now, i will fathom. i will imagine. i will do this.

for Him. for *us*. for our *family*.

my first time.

i am nervous, but eager to participate. to contribute. to be an active member of the family, our family, *my* family.

shelly is going to show me the ropes.

this is reassuring to me. shelly and i have, after all, shared nearly everything that two people can share.

we are almost the same body, shelly and i. almost blood. we are true *sisters*. so i am relieved that she is the one to shelter me, to show me the ropes.

she nods at me. "remember to smile."

she grins, part demonstration, part genuine

emotion. she throws back her shoulders, reminding me of the soft goosefleshed skin that ripples beneath her thin top. reminding me of another reason why people want to give her things.

why people want to fill her up.

"the busboys. the runners. they can't resist," she says. "that's why Henry sends the girls. and, i mean, they have so much left over, the restaurants. at the end of the day. they have so much *extra*."

it is the end of the day. we are cloaked in dusk, dusted in the first sprinklings of starlight.

the idea, the notion that there could be extra? could be more? could be *infinite*?

it is dizzying, dazzling. it makes me feel drunk with fullness, makes me feel fizzy, makes me feel like small sprinkles of starlight. makes me feel like dusk, taking hold.

shelly raps on the back-door exit of the restaurant. after a moment, a smooth, brown-skinned face appears.

small, round eyes drink shelly in as she keeps her shoulders pressing back, keeps her smile pasted to her face, keeps in mind the family. the *extra*. the *infinite*.

they exchange a few words, a meaningful glance, and then the brown-skinned boy disappears back into the restaurant.

i panic briefly. what would Henry do if we were to fail? if we were to come home empty-handed?

we can't. *i* can't. there is no letting Henry down. there is no disappointing Henry.

the boy returns, this time with a paper grocery bag balanced in the crook of each elbow.

my entire body, my entire *being*, sighs. shudders with the relief of success.

outside of the car, shelly shows me our bounty: sacks of rice, day-old vegetables only beginning to turn, lettuce wrinkling weakly at the edges. meat that should freeze well.

so much. *extra.*

i ask what would have happened if no one had come to the door, if the brown-skinned boy hadn't wanted to help us.

she points to the two tall metal dumpsters planted at the far end of the parking lot.

"there's plenty in there," she says. "you'd be surprised."

but i wouldn't. i wouldn't be surprised. i can't be surprised, anymore.

i *get* it now.

now, i know.

you wouldn't believe the sorts of things that some people throw away.

you wouldn't.

but i would.

human beings waste all kinds of things.

back inside of the car, shelly clasps my hand under hers. we wrap our fingers over the worn gearshift of the pickup.

"Henry is going to be impressed," she assures me. "Henry is going to be proud. of you."

her fingers are warm, they hum with energy, and i cannot think of another time, of a *before*, of any other member of my *family*
    <no mother i never had a father>
who knew what it was to be proud. of *me*.
to *love. me.*

but no matter.
that is why, as Henry explains, there *is* no *before.*

only *now.* only *infinity.*
only the *undertow.*
and me,
adrift.

legend

the story goes:

    Henry's mother once traded Him for a pitcher of beer.

    i don't learn this from Henry, of course; Henry never speaks of the *before*, any *before*, and certainly not His own.

    if you ask Henry, He has no parents. He has shaken off His too-tight skin, shed His ego, rejected all but the *now*.

    but still:

    the story. *goes*. it breathes. it gathers its own momentum. it weaves its way about the ranch, snakes through, wiggles underneath doorjambs, presses flat against windowsills, shimmies from ear to listening ear.

    shelly is the one who finally shares it with me.

    my listening ear may well be the last to be bent. some of the others here on the ranch still keep me at arm's length, still seal themselves off from me, curl themselves tightly in their own cling-wrap casings. leila is too distrustful, too creased with anger. junior is too preoccupied with the gaping chasm of his cavernous *wants*.

    some of the others still see me as other. and i, them.

    thank goodness Henry's love is enough to make up the difference, to fill up the hollow, empty spaces.

family

enough. *more* than enough. *so much* more.

thank goodness Henry's love is free.

some of the others still see me as other. and i,
them.

but shelly? shelly will share *anything*. she will share
anything with *me*.

that is why we are sisters, shelly and i. that is why
we are closer than paper dolls, tighter than stitches on
a quilt.

that is why shelly and i are nearly blood.

shelly will share anything. with *me*. and she does.

and so, she does.

"a pitcher of *beer*." she leans forward on sharp
elbows, mouth puckered in a perfect *o* of disbelief.

we are shucking ears of corn for dinner, heaps,
mountains, towers of corn. we work in quiet
synchronicity, bent over a splintering wooden picnic
table, peeling thick hunks of corn silk back from the
grainy, raw pearls of butter-pale kernel.

we toss the empty husks into a large metal garbage
bin pushed to the side of our table.

the trash quickly piles up.

i roll flosslike strands of corn silk between my
thumb and forefinger, thoughtful.

beer.

"*beer*," she repeats, though i have not spoken aloud.

(that is how close, how connected shelly and i are.

she hears the things i have only said on the inside. she *is* my inside. that is how close we are. sisters. near-blood.)

"*beer.*"

she repeats it with shrill outrage, spits the word past her lips as though it were poison. as though it is *beer* that is the real issue here. as though there were something else, some other substance for which Henry could have been traded that might make more sense, that might be acceptable.

as though there were any excuse for voluntarily giving up Henry.

she doesn't look at me, can't see the fury that i feel molding, melting into my features. but she can feel it.

(because she is my insides, my secret spaces. because we are connected.)

"she was, um, a waitress," she goes on. "and i guess she drank?"

i guess.

"and Henry was with her one day, at work? i think He was still pretty little back then. like maybe six or seven or something like that."

i cannot reconcile the notion of a young-boy Henry. there is too much Henry, so much, a watershed of Henry, to think that there had ever been less.

no.

"she had some friend, some other waitress, a woman who couldn't have kids no matter how hard she tried. it was real sad," shelly says, like she knew this woman personally, was well acquainted with her sorrows, with her hollowed-out core, with her *wants*.

"so the story goes that they were drinking, you know, once they'd finished their shifts? and after a few too many, this friend, this woman? she offered Henry's mom a pitcher of beer in exchange for taking Him home.

"and Henry's mom agreed to it."

she agreed to it. agreed.

who could ever do that? who could ever give up Henry?

no.

i feel a small rumble, a tickle at the back of my throat. before i even realize that i am going to speak, the words are there:

"so how did He—?"

it is perfunctory, my question. shelly is deep, lost in the legend. she is reflecting inward, talking mainly with her own mirror-self. i can see this. all i need to do is sit silently, to open my listening ear. to *be* her mirror-self. the way that she is mine.

i can do that. that, i can do.

"an uncle. or something. came to pick Him up a few days later."

a few days later.
days.

so.
assuming this story is true:
how many days?
how many days later?
when was the decision made to retrieve Henry?
what changed people's minds?
and what happened to Him, during that gray-
space, that squishy, unspoken time that he was pent up,
smothered, caged in with that woman and her wants?
assuming the story is true.

assuming that—that the story is true, that this
is a sequence of events in which Henry was genuinely
involved—assuming all of these things, i will still never
know.

i will never, ever know for certain. because for
all that Henry is an endless well of love, He is just as
much a vault, airtight, snug with His own secrets of an
unknown, never-to-be-known, *before.*

still: saved by "an uncle." this is what shelly says.
she lays a small, tanned hand flat against the picnic
table with the quiet, calm confidence of an insider's
knowledge.
i think of "uncle" jack, who was not, is not, will
never be my uncle.
it is nice to know—comforting, like a glass of

ice water at midafternoon, like the confidence of an
insider—it is a relief, really to know:

to know that uncles can be good for something.

a pitcher of beer.

a pitcher. of *beer.*

you wouldn't believe the sorts of things that some
people throw away.

human beings waste all kinds of things.

singer

the singer is a living doll, the human embodiment of barbie.

she possesses the sort of flawless, breathless, intricate beauty that pulls like a fist, sucks at you with wonder, leaves you mute with dazzlement.

she is ethereal.

she is perfection.

she is

doomed.

the singer is also alone.

it isn't that she has no *family*. no, not quite.

but rather: her husband, someone blank and important, is away. he travels often, the burden of being blank and important.

while he is gone, she sets about preparing for everything that is to come. for their life together. for their sometime family.

her husband is a music manager. he fulfills other people's fantasies. he makes his money by spreading other people's messages, their love.

their house is new to them, a gift from husband to wife. a nest for her, for the singer—to feather, to fill with light and sun and warmth.

while her husband is away, the singer sets about preparing.

she has friends who look in on her. many friends: gentle, caring people, people who stop by for an afternoon, an evening, or a week yet. there is room for them, so much room in the house. so much love and space and everyone.

she isn't lonely, feels connected and cared for even in the void of her husband's absence. she spends late afternoons smiling, stretched out across overstuffed sofas, sipping at warm, comforting, innocuous things like herbal tea. communicating soundlessly with her houseguests, luxuriating in her exquisite *everything*. feeling secure, sound, safe.

i don't know the singer—beyond what i've seen in magazines, that is—and i certainly don't know her husband. her houseguests. i imagine if i'd thought about it, i would have recognized her life, her *orbit*, as something far-reaching. magnetic.

something like the *something* for which Henry searches.

for now, though—

in the *now*—

Henry's spotlight still skates the boundaries of her universe.

for *now*.

for now, her *infinity*, her *everything*, is light-years from my own, from any i've ever experienced. her house is sprawling, feathered and fluffed, stuffed to the brim with love and light and *so much*.

so. much.

i don't yet know, think i might never know, how
Henry came upon this house, this woman, this parallel
universe. this in-between space, where warmth is a
welcoming bath rather than a raging fever, where gentle
friends weave themselves to you just when you are
feeling frayed. where wire gates block out the ugliness of
the outside world.

where there are steel barriers to press up against
the vortex, the orbit, the black hole.

where there are fences, systems, codes of security,
and soundless safety. where there are endless, infinite,
effortless means.

where there are countless ways to hold the
undertow at bay.

Henry says: everything belongs to everyone.
Henry says: there is no *i*. no *ego*. no need for parents.
Henry says: there is only *family*. our family.

but:
Henry has a message, of love and light and music.
and He is searching for people, for open, yielding
souls
to spread His word.

Henry is the one who found the singer.

after

the singer struggles.

she strains, breaks, thrashes against the current, digs her heels into the *now*.

she heaves, hiccups, twists with pain, bright and swift.

she bleeds.

i listen to sounds.

they come to me, unbidden.

choked, thick, drenched with helplessness, they come to me.

unbidden.

the singer pleads, cries, begs. wants to live.

she moans.

her voice is soft, but somehow still unmistakable amidst the deafening mayhem. it rises above the screaming, gaping, oozing chaos. i hear her. shelly hears her. there is no way to not-hear her.

she seeps. from somewhere deep, someplace inescapable.

she is, suddenly, *everything*.

i shudder, stagger, heave. i shut my eyes, open them again.

i take in shelly.

my sister, my secret, inside self—shelly.

i see her. take her in.

she is hovering, poised above the singer, who is little more than a husk of herself, really, little more than her own half-life.

the singer is emptying out. hollowing.

maybe shelly is, too. maybe we all are.

maybe this is our *now*, the *now* that we have finally come to, collectively, pedaling furiously, foolishly.

paddling directly into the eye of the storm.

shelly pauses, wipes the back of her palm against her forehead, leaving a streak of rust-colored blood stark against the blank expanse of her pale skin.

she is marked. she is endless. she is forever.

she is *now*.

i want. i *so* want:

i want to take the entire broken, bleeding household. the singer and her friends, her *family*.

i want to scoop up all of the bodies—gentle bodies, now rendered limp and life-drained. to close the chasm between *here*, *now*, and *infinity*. to ground them. to keep them afloat.

i *want*.

inside.

my hands are streaked with blood that is not my own.

inside, past the threshold. but still, somehow apart.

my hands are streaked with blood that is not my own, and the horror-movie sound effects persist.

< . . . >

interference

white noise.

torrents of skin and bone.

skin and bone, and blood. so much blood.

rushes, tidal waves, well-deep reflecting pools of blood, raging everywhere, catching in every corner, flickering and taking hold like a thick, coppery fever.

i burn.

i melt.

i sink.

i drown.

bodies.

there are bodies everywhere. and the bodies are broken.

we are all broken. we are all supernovas. black holes, disintegrating.

we are all crushing, pulling, recoiling, unraveling.

we are all collapsing in on ourselves,
like dying stars.

part II

never

i never did believe in heaven.
    if i had, after all, perhaps then, *then*, i would have
embraced my own infinity, once upon a time back
home, in my mother's anti-fantasy; perhaps i wouldn't
have welcomed the cascade, the tidal wave, the rushing
torrents of pills.
    perhaps then, i would have let go of the *now*.

    but.
    to me, *afterlife* has always sounded like an
oxymoron, like the type of dirty trick the
    cloud-shapes,
    the cloud-shifts—
    the creeping, smothering cloud covers—
    the type of trick they play on your mind during
those moments.
    during those brief interludes
    when you dare to let your guard
    down.

    afterlife is little more than the broken promise, the
unfulfilled premise of something intangible,
    something ephemeral.
    something like a wisp, a whisper;
    something like the unfathomable suggestion

family

of a whole and perfect day.
a blink. a hiccup. imperceptible.
a violation of the tidy, tidal, either/or.

afterlife is like the undertow:
always pressing, churning, roiling.
but never *now*. never realized.

never, not ever, something to rely upon.

i never did believe in heaven.
i am still not completely sure of what i think
of hell.

after

"it's time, mel. get dressed."

    my eyelids flutter.
    i struggle, briefly. thrash against the hour. strain
to pierce the eggshell-thin, frail, fragile veil between
conscious and light, between coma and wake.
    between *now* and *infinity.*

    i have a stupefying moment of *who/where/how*, and
then realize all at once, in a dizzying rush, a flood of *yes.*

    oh. *yes.*
    a barrage of *come to now.*
    i realize:
    it is time.

    i cough, press my palms hard against the
open-slatted floor, feel the ridges, the grooves and
indentations, feel so much past-life, history, so much
before, burrowed, carved deep beneath the surface.
    i stretch back from my mattress, rise. my bones
make a hollow, creaking sound as i stand, shaking off
sleep.
    the creaking, the pops and hiccups, they startle me.
they are the sounds of my skeleton snapping into place,
the sounds of my skin, bone, sinew, settling. of my

pockets, my pieces, my shadow spaces, expanding and contracting with my every bated breath.

they are the sounds of my body reshaping itself, readying itself.

reeling.

they are the sounds of the opposite of solid.

it is time.
it is late. it is the witching hour.

junior's face hovers, inches from my own.

i sense him, feel the edges of his skin ooze, radiate, pulsate with energy, with anticipation, with *yes, now, always.*

junior *wants.*

it is the type of *want* you could clutch, you could grasp; the type of *want* you could wind around a crooked finger.

through the tar-thick, viscous cover of night, i can feel it, the *want*, constricting across my shoulders, weaving about my collarbones like a frayed noose. i can inhale and breathe his *want* into me so fiercely that i can almost taste its rancor.

can almost pretend it's my own.

almost.

it has been too long, here on the ranch. here in ersatz-everything, here without windows, without edges, without

<interference>

far too long.

so much so, *so* long, that it has begun to feel that our *infinity*, our collective orbit, might be fading. losing shape, strength, elasticity.

might be fraying.

might be washing away like an etching in the sand as the tide comes in and slowly, steadily—but irreversibly—erases what once was. leaves only the *now*. unwinds, unravels infinity, indefinitely.

i am not surprised to realize this.
after all, infinity has always felt impossible to me.

there is nothing, after all, that doesn't end.

concert

Henry is our preacher, our anchor, our window.
    He tells us the gospel, according to
    Him.
    (as if there were any other version than His. as if
there could ever be.)

    His favorite sermons are those that tell of unity, of
harmony, of a message carried by music. He pens His
own lilting rifts;
    His scores reverberate,
    punctuate the rise
    and fall
    of all of our hours.
    together.

    His melodies are our hymns, and every day that we
sing with Him,
    for Him,
    we are supplicant.
    we are one.
    family.

    still.
    Henry's music, His message, it is too powerful,
    too bright and wide to be contained.

He—*we all*—want to share it. to sing it to the people. to the entire vast, expanding universe.
   in concert.

   Henry loves a concert. He *does*.
   it is the only piece of the *then*, the ever-*before*, that He is willing, even eager, to dwell upon. to share with us.
   music is a collective history, a catechism that unites.
   music is Henry's *always*, the way that mirror-mel and uncle jack and
   <*not my mother no mother never*>
   all of the stages of the rolling tide
   are my own.

   the way that they mark my own inner history,
   the way that they echo a refrain that only i can hear.

   Henry's favorite story is a sunken treasure of a memory. it is a tableau that becomes more vivid with each retelling, becomes an out-loud fact, a sensory reality.
   something that envelopes us, orbits us.
   all of us.

   Henry loves the story of woodstock.
   He tells us: woodstock was an overrun concert, held in an open field on a borrowed farm.

it was free love and music and magic.
crowds, clouds, consciousness.
and bodies.
gentle bodies, tangles of hair, skin against skin as
the rain beat down.
one family, open, warm, receptive.

and when Henry speaks
<preaches>
i *hear* Him.
see myself there.
can see, so clearly, so sharply, why music is Henry's
message.

i can see
how:
for a boy who was once traded
for a pitcher of *beer*
<you wouldn't believe>
<human beings waste>
the notion of woodstock—
of bodies and warmth and
harmony—
it must have been:
a welcome hum
of promise.
a *premise*—
an ancient premonition
of how He would eventually come to

conduct
<orchestrate>
our life on the ranch.

"woodstock was a message," He explains, "and
people heard it. the *man* heard it."
woodstock was unique, the sort of experience that
created shifts,
swift and nearly imperceptible.

woodstock is like Henry:
self-contained. ephemeral.
magnetic.

Henry has His own message, of course.
His own music, His own magic.
His own love.

and people will hear it.

love and terror

Henry has designs.

  Henry has thoughts about being famous, being
real, being
    important.
    being noticed.
    <as though>
    as though there were someone who could possibly
not notice Henry.
    as though there were
    anything, anywhere, *anyone*
    other than Henry.

  He has ideas. one idea, specifically.
    He wants to start a band.
    not simply your standard folk music, understand;
Henry's band would be more than our mingled voices
gathered at the campfire.
    more than our words, our sounds, our songs,
intertwining with the plumes of smoke, the lapping
flames, the spreading heat.
    the fever.
    it would be more. *so much* more.
    it would be His word, His truth,
    gospel.
    it would be *everything.*

micol ostow

because *Henry* is *everything.*
and *He* will always,
always
need
more.

Henry's band—our *family's* band—
our word, our truth,
it would spread
wide as woodstock.
wider than any moment from
anyone's
ever *before.*

Henry says that music is love. and terror.
Henry knows. always. everything. He *knows.*

and so.
there is a certain terror amongst us, the members
of His family; a fear that comes from the suspicion that
Henry will always need more—
more than *us,*
more than we are,
more than we can ever be.
He needs a platform, wide as woodstock,
wider than the infinite ocean.
wider than our family's orbit, we fear.

and so

we sing
for Him.

in love.
(and fear)
we sing.
for Him.

windows

we have no windows to the outside world.

    here on the ranch, we are self-contained, like russian dolls nesting each within a larger hollow. we fill each other up, fit snugly inside each other's membranes, each other's open spaces.

    we link. we interlock.

    and *we* are all that we all need.

    for always.

    Henry says, "everything belongs to everyone."

    still, He is the only one allowed to watch the television set.

    He is the only one of us with access, with passage, with a window to the outside world.

    He is the only one with contact, with connection.

    with *interference*.

    as He should be.

    we know: He shields us for our own protection. out of respect. love. like a father would.

    He shares, of course.

    (of course.)

    of course, He shares the meaningful news with us. He assures us of this. He is careful to pass along any information with meaning.

as though there could be meaning without Henry
to imbue it.

(as though.)

but. He does. share.

this, we trust.

(in Henry, we trust.)

He is our father. our everyone.

He is our window.

chosen

in our family, we are each of us special. unique.
treasured.
    but.
    there is such a thing as being *more* treasured than
the rest,
    more wanted, for a time.
    there is such a thing as being
    chosen.

    Henry's orbit is vast.
    there is *so much* Henry that He can handpick a
handmaiden, can select one sister with whom to fuse
from time to time.
    one person to be the closest to Him of us all.

    often, it is leila or shelly who are called to wrap
themselves within Henry's cocoon. they are the sisters
who have been with Him the longest, who have proven
themselves worthy of His trust and glory.
    often, it is leila or shelly.
    but tonight, i am called.
    tonight, *i* am chosen.
    special.
    i am Henry's. i alone.
    i am
    loved.

i am Henry's tonight, alone. and so, tonight, my broken edges are oh-so-slightly sanded down.

tonight, i am Henry's, and i am slightly more whole.

this is what it means to be
chosen.

He approaches me just after dinner.

i am rising to head toward the oversize basins and faucets housed in the barn—to rinse dishes, to render things clean once again—when Henry appears behind me.

though i cannot see Him from where He stands, His presence is immediately felt. something happens to the air, the atmosphere, when Henry approaches; all of the tiny cells and particles that bind together to create my being stand on point when He arrives. i shudder and contract, shiver as He lays a warm palm against the nape of my neck.

"will you come back with me tonight?"

i nod, weak. unable to form words.

of course.

of *course* i will go back with Henry to His private space, His sanctum. it is an honor, a gift, to be chosen.

tonight, for a time, i am
special.
unique.
almost whole.

i quickly finish rinsing my dinner plate and return

it to its shelf with the rest of our family's dishware. i rub my hands against the front of my drawstring skirt and head toward the entrance to the barn.

my body, my bones hum with anticipation, with fever.

i burn.

i am on my way to His room.

i have been chosen.

the other sisters know, can tell what it means when Henry appears from behind that way, a look of devout reverence etched across His features. like me, they quiver, despite being the ones who, for tonight, at least, have been overlooked. like me, they crackle with energy and fire.

we are a chain of paper dolls, after all, and all connected. we are conjoined, one unit, despite my being *chosen* for the night.

shelly grabs at me as i pass her by, pinches the soft flesh above my hip. i look back at her and she grins at me.

her expression shows no trace of jealousy or anger. no betrayal. my sister, my paper-doll partner, she *knows* as well as any of them, understands that Henry's love is overflowing. that there is more than enough for each of us.

time enough for us all, each of us,

to be chosen.

hideaway

Henry's room is a hideaway.

it is a comforting cave, a nest.

His quarters are set apart from our own bunks, our
rows of unrolled sleeping bags laid out; a chaotic quilt
across the dusty floor of one of the outbuildings of the
barn. Henry stays in the general store, up closer to the
front entrance to the ranch, closer to where emmett
lives.

closer to the boundary between our haven and the
real world.

He is our window, after all.

Henry's room is a sanctuary, a haven, but reveals
no details about His before, His true core. being invited
into His private spaces does not grant access to His
innermost mind.

even here, nestled against Him, veiled by the
fragile gauze of His lazily draped bedsheets, awash
in the heady scent of Him—even here, *now*, He is a
mystery.

"what do you think?" He asks.

i think: no man has ever asked for my opinion
before. has ever cared. but then, Henry knows that.
Henry *knows*. everything.

i smile slowly. take it all in: the splintering grooves
that run deep into the wooden plank walls, the vibrant

tapestries He's hung. even something as ordinary as the worn rubber sole of His overturned sandal peeking out from underneath a corner of the bed frame, even that small detail seems holy in the *now*.

everything about Henry is holy. everything He touches.

and so.

i tilt, turn my body toward His, searching. i beg Him, with widened eyes, to put His hands on me. to touch *me*.

to make *me*

holy.

and whole.

choir

Henry is our window, and our rudder. He is the one of us with access, with any window to the outside world.

but He shares. with us. He does.

and tonight, He shares with *me*.

after we have fused, connected, healed each other—after He has put His hands on me and made me holy—He tells me stories. fanciful tales, legends

<*the story goes . . .*>

from a collective *before*,

a moment when music was power.

i rest my head against His bare chest, tracing the grooves, the valleys and fault lines of His skin. take hold of the smoky wand of magic cloud that He extends between two graceful fingers. i inhale, adrift. searching for consciousness.

awaiting.

Henry's stories, the tales He shares, are about bodies, mostly. bodies breaking apart and coming back together. bodies that connect and then shatter. gentle, fragmented bodies, ready for a message. *His* message.

and music. Henry's favorite stories are about music, and the messages that it carries.

one day He—
we—
our *family*—
will have a story of our own. to sing out.
to share.

His skin pressed against my own, Henry begins one
of His most-loved tales, one He's shared with me before,
though never quite like this, never just the two of us.
the story, though familiar, feels different with His heart
pulsing against me. His body beats out its own metered
rhythm, lulling me.

Henry tells me another truth about the power of
music to
  reach,
  to preach
  to envelop.
  to entwine.
  a story about
  a message set to
  spoil.
  a story about
  a message gone
  sour.

"a concert," He says, waving His free arm languidly.
"lots of performers.
it was supposed to be a celebration.
supposed to be about love and light.

but it went bad.
"that would never happen to us.
to our family.

"we're gonna get our music out there," He says.
"spread our message.
one day.
you'll see."

i believe it, of course.
of course, i believe it.
Henry's word is gospel.
and my sisters and i,
His faithful choir.

i sidle closer still, until we are so tightly pressed
together that we might be breathing from the same
lungs. i gaze up at Henry with wide-eyed worship.
tilt my body toward Him, rest a tentative hand on His
knee.
i open my hollow spaces to Him. it may be that i
am not His only grateful supplicant.
<far from it.>
so far. *infinity*. light-years away.
but. tonight, *i* am here, alone. *i* am chosen.
tonight, His stories are for
me.

Henry's love is full to bursting. overflowing.

Henry's love is torrents, tides. raging fevers of *always*.
He burns.
we *all* burn.
the whole world is
<*endless infinite always*>
burning.

but tonight
my world
is
still.

chaos

i want to know.
    burn to know.
    alone, with Henry, in His bed, i need to hear. to
learn. from Henry.
    about a time when a message went sour.
    about a time when the love and light
    transformed
    into something filthy and fetid.
    about a time
    that turned.
    that went
    bad.

    i ask, "what happened?"

Henry makes a deep, choked sound, something
between a laugh and something else; a noise more full,
more round, more
    <inescapable>
    supple.
    "people forget," He says.
    "people don't want to think about stuff like that."
    <bodies, fever, rushing, crushing, tides>

    He says:
    "it was chaos. total chaos."

His eyes glitter. His body shudders.

there is something about the word: *chaos.*
something fierce.

chaos.

the word slithers, undulates, winds its way down
Henry's spine. i can see it growing, gathering speed,
strength, silent power. i can see Henry straighten
against the backboard of the bed.

i can see it burrow deep, lodge itself within His
fault lines.

<*chaos*>

chaos is a fierce thing.

Henry purses His lips. swallows forcefully. brushes
a wild thatch of hair from His eyes.

"too many people, getting riled. and security got
out of control.

the crew—

the men that were hired to keep the peace—

they got violent with the crowd.

lots of folks were injured. some died."

some died.

a bitter taste builds up inside of me, rises to the
back of my throat. i look down, away, reach for a glass
of water.

i think: *violence.*
i think: *bodies.*

crushing, reaching, stretching bodies.
feverish, electric bodies, roiling and churning.
bodies pulled by an invisible undertow.
bodies rushing toward the *now*, toward the
half-life.
toward a collective, unknown,
afterlife.

bodies. so many bodies. too many.
torrents of skin and bone.
skin and bone, and blood.

Henry shakes His head, makes the guttural sound
again. "that this would happen at a concert. a *concert*.
don't people know?
music is the message.
music is how we spread our word.
music is how we share our love."

music.
Henry's music will reach, expand, fill. it will creep
toward all the bodies and seep into the empty places.
Henry's music, His message—it is *always*, *now*,
forever.
it is *infinity*.
and it will be heard.

"music and chaos are two separate things," Henry
continues, more to Himself than to me, now.

He repeats: "two separate things." this is an important point. a point worth sharing.
this is a point that has *meaning*.

He is right, of course. He *is*. right.
He is always right.
music is love.
Henry is love.

but *chaos*?
chaos is a fierce thing.
chaos burrows deep.

in the *now*

life on the ranch is not very chaotic.
    chaos is outside.

    we are taught: there is no *i*, no *ego*, no *before*.
    we are taught: there is only the *now*.
    but *in* the now: there are routines. there are
rhythms. there is a steadiness to be found.

    namely, there are chores.
    every day of every week, chores. we divide the
tasks amongst ourselves, the *family*.
    some days i am sent, usually with shelly, to forage
for food.

    foraging can be okay because i like to ride in the
pickup, like to feel the smooth, sturdy motion of rubber
tires beneath me, to watch the horizon race along
against my sight line,
    just forever out of reach,
    just forever limitless.

    i like to soak, to simmer, in the air outside the
ranch, which is somehow, sometimes, crisper, brighter,
cleaner.
    more.
    even when we are knee-deep in day-old produce.

i like to be with my sister, shelly.
i like to provide for my
family.

still, the truth is:
shelly is a lot.
she is. a *lot*. to take.
and in the smooth, sturdy safe house of the pickup,
there is only me to take her.
in those moments, we have no buffer between us,
she and i.
how lucky it is, then, that we are sisters. that we are
so close we are nearly one person, nearly fit neatly into
one set of skin, our thoughts occurring almost in tandem.
shelly is my inside-out. my mirror-me. my shadow-
self. she wears her fault lines on the outside, trophies
pinned to the heavy cloak of her self.
whereas everything, every last bit of me, all of my
hollow places—they are wrapped up tightly and stuffed
down inside.
shelly is the inner voice that i dare not allow to speak
aloud. she is fire, shattered glass, and shards of ice. she is
her own orbit, her own atmosphere. her own half-life.
shelly and mirror-mel
<*mirror*-me>—
they wear their scar tissue like bright, shiny
ribbons. like prizes.
they embrace their fractures, swallow their chaos
whole.

while i am merely
broken.

shelly has opinions about everything. but shelly's
everything is quite specific; usually her opinions, her
points of reference—usually they snake their way back
to Henry. always Henry.

and even though i *get it*, i really do

<—*Henry is* always; *sometimes just the suggestion of
Henry awake, alive in my mind fills me up so i think i could
die for Him just from thinking about it*—>

even though i *get it*, it is a lot.

today, now, in the cramped cab of the pickup, it is
almost too much. the glaze that falls over her eyes and
the rote movement of her lips, they unsettle me, make
me think of painted dolls, of static.

of blankness.

it is . . . upsetting. shelly is my inside-out, my
positive charge.

but today, shelly has hollow places. *so many* hollow
places.

and today, she shows them to me.

today, her
fault lines
are beginning
to
crack.

mothers

i cannot not ask.

i need to know what it is that has shelly so blank, so fully distracted. she is cracking, crumbling, and there should be no secrets among *family*, i reason. not *our* family.

so. i venture:

"what is it?"

shelly's cheeks flush, pink bloom creeping up toward her temples like a rash, but her gaze doesn't leave the road. "you can tell?"

"of course."

of *course*. of course i can. she is me. she is my shadow-self. i *know*.

"it's—" she falters, pressing her lips together until they are little more than a thin white line. her cheekbones set into sharp angles, hollow and haunted.

i place a hand against her knee, reassuring her. she can say anything to me, i remind her. she *is* me.

she nods, almost to herself, winds her arms and runs the steering wheel all the way to the right, driving us off to the side of the road, to a soft shoulder, where we finally settle.

the engine sputters and the truck falls silent.

she turns to me, her face a jigsaw puzzle that's been

forced together incorrectly, tabs jutting from too-tight cutouts.

"i'm going to have a baby."

there is a hitch, a hiccup, and a trapdoor opens at the base of my stomach.

she is pregnant.

shelly is *pregnant*.

i soar downward, into the vortex where the floor has given way beneath me.

this. is incomprehensible.

i am overwhelmed.

overjoyed.

shelly is pregnant.

i am overjoyed.

shelly is growing a new life inside of her. her body is a safe house,

a haven.

our family will have a new baby.

our sisters will be mothers.

and Henry will always be our father.

this baby, the very fact of it—

it means that the fabric of our family is now that much more firmly woven, that much more inextricable. the surface of our puzzle pieces have been brushed with glue.

we are bound.
eternal.
infinite.

my eyes shine. i scrabble across the seat, clutch shelly tightly. her body feels rigid against my own.

i understand: she is afraid.

she is not the first of our sisters to give birth on the ranch, not hardly, but she is the sister who is my own second skin.

her fear is natural. but this news, this new life—it is something to celebrate.

of this, i am certain.

and so, i tell her so: "you aren't alone. this baby is all of ours."

there is no ego, no *i*, no before, i remind her. no parents. just us: the family. infinity, and love, and binding. the sins of the fathers have been washed from the slate. we are clean, scrubbed and fresh. we, our *family*—we can create our own *now*. a *now* for the baby.

shelly's baby. all of ours.

it is a miracle.

i never did believe in heaven, and yet.

it *is*.

a miracle.

she hears me, allows my thrill to shower her. i can see that she hears me.

a clarity comes over those storm-cloud eyes.

she takes a breath, nods. "i'm not worried; that's
not the right word.
it's just, i can't"—
she bites at her lip—
"the father could be anyone.
junior, Henry . . . or someone else.
it could be anyone else from the ranch."

she looks ashamed, looks the way i sometimes felt
after a visit with uncle jack—
like a nuclear rain shower couldn't begin
to undo the stains.
but why? because the baby could be anyone's?
as though that even mattered.
as though that weren't the entire point of our life,
together, on the ranch.
our *family*.

"but we are all *one* family," i insist.
"we are *all* Henry's children, wives, and sisters.
everything—every*one*—belongs to everybody."
"true."
though she still sounds uncertain, my enthusiasm
must have leaked, spilled over past the edges of her
body's boundaries. she hazards a hopeful grin. reaches
out, clasps her fingers around my own.
"we can do this," she offers, more as a question
than a statement.

"Henry—He has connections, contacts.
there's a man He met, sometime back,
a music manager.
someone important.
this guy's gonna come out, hear us sing, take a
listen to Henry's stuff.
help us get the message out."

i nod, knowing:
Henry's reach, His grasp, is far.
His orbit is infinite.
His connections like sticky spider-webbing.

"it's gonna mean money," shelly goes on. "for the
baby. for our *family.*"

i blink.
money.
of course,
babies—
people—
families—
cost
money.

we live so well on cast-offs,
on *trash.*
that i had nearly forgotten about

such real-world things.
things like
money.

i have a moment,
a hiccup,
where the soft spaces of my throat seem to tighten,
to close.
where mirror-mel awakens,
wide-eyed,
wondering:

<money>

wondering:
what ever happened
to free love?

but mirror-mel
should know better
than to question Henry.

"we can do this," shelly says again,
and the choking,
closing
<drowning>
sensation
melts away.

i turn to shelly.
my *sister.*
soon to be a *mother.*

i nod, utterly convinced.
"of course we can.
we *will.*

"we're *family.*"

uncle

Henry says, there is no *before*, and He is right.

He knows. everything. sees right through people
like they're cut from glass, His eyes the prism of a
psychic kaleidoscope: telepathic, all-knowing.
infinite.

i have no *before*, no memory of what it was to have
a father.
no memory of life before the undertow, before
eternity overtook me.
before *infinity.*

but.

there is one thought,
one mind-image,
one flash of consciousness that can't be erased,
no matter the cloudy bursts i breathe in,
no matter how my lungs fill of Henry's medicine,
of magic smoke
that i suck down
into the empty, decaying base of my body:

there is the day that i met my uncle.
jack.

i was small.

i was small, and my father only ever a pencil tracing, a paper cutout, a shadow of a concept that my mother whispered to herself

in those moments that she happened to forget herself.

to forget *me*.

my father was, near as i could tell, a wisp of an afterthought,

a fleeting prayer, mumbled incoherently.

a suggestion of a sketch, buried deep within the footnotes of my mother's life plan.

mother wasn't one for planning. and so. i never had a father.

only uncle jack.

"mel," mother said, leaning forward. the heavy vapors of her scent clogged and clotted at the back of my throat, choking me off, strangling me.

"this is jack. he's going to stay with us for a while."

and the look in his eyes—

a gleam that suggested that he understood the depths of my own transparency—

that was enough, *more* than enough, to still a girl my age,

then barely five years old.

"you can call me uncle."

his breath reeked of alcohol and secrets.
of rot and undertow
and promises
unfulfilled.

i knew:
there was something about a girl who hadn't ever
known her father;
there were words for that fractured outline of a
person, words hurled at me by playground passersby,
people who couldn't possibly have grasped the strength
of the cloying showers of hatred they spewed.

i was small, still. barely five years old.
i was something dirty. undeserving.
something barely of this world.

i understood, even then, what it was to be lacking.
what it was to have a gaping, yawning hole—a
chasm where one's *family* should be.
it was a
punch line
that for once, i was in on.
even then.
even small.

there was something about a girl who didn't have a
father.
something rotted,

set to
spoil.

uncle jack wasn't going to change that.
he had his own empty places.
hollow spaces.
and it was clear to me,
even then,
even small,

that he
had
his own plans
to fill
those fault lines
up.

home

when shelly and i return home with the fruits of our
foraging, leila is in the kitchen.
    lately, leila is often in the kitchen.
    and i often like to stay away from leila.
    lately.
    lately, i stay
    away.

    lately, she and junior tilt their heads together,
exchange glances like their insides are radios tuned to
the same frequency.
    lately, there are whispers, conversational lilts that
ring like hushed, muffled music.
    there are revved engines, lately,
    and headlights that wash over the charred remains
of our campfire hours after we've snuffed the flames
and headed off to sleep.
    it is . . . unsettling.
    so.
    lately, i stay away from leila as best i can.
    which means staying out of the kitchen.

    it is wrong, i know, to avoid her. to avoid junior.
    they are, both of them,
    my *family*.
    but.

i am not the only one grappling with uncertainty.
i think back to shelly's delicate trembling,
her hesitation
back in the pickup
<*the baby could be anyone's*>.

there is a certain amount of
uncertainty.

even here, among Henry's watersheds, His
bottomless caches of love and light.
even here, there are moments of doubt,
of afterthought
and undertow.

it may be wrong, but regardless:
it is fierce.
deep.

inescapable.

teeth

leila bares her teeth.

    when shelly and i enter the kitchen, arms bowing
under the weight of our bounty, there is a moment—
    a slight,
    nearly imperceptible,
    sliver of a second—
    that leila's teeth are exposed:

white,
the shade of sun-bleached bone.

    her face is an expansive mask of hunger.
    her angles have been sharpened to precision.

    i think of shelly, of her soft vulnerability,
    of the extra heartbeat that pulses
    through the road maps of her body.
    we exchange a glance—
    shelly,
    my *sister*,
    and i—
    a moment of mutual transparency—
    and come to a tacit agreement.

    she shuffles the grocery bags against her hips,

micol ostow

gives no hint of the other cargo
she totes.

the baby is our secret.

it may belong to our family—
<no ego no i>
to all of us—

but for now, it is still
our secret.

after

leila is dressed in black:
    black jeans, black boots, slim black turtleneck
pulled over her taut, slender frame.
    she is a spring-loaded coil, coated in ink. she is
slick, she is thick, she is heavy with sinister expectation.
    she is the execution of a plot, a plan.
    a threat.
    hollow need hangs from her.
    want drips from her limbs, caresses her joints,
pools within her crevasses, her cracks, her rivulets.
    she brims, bursts,
    overflows with *now*.
    her half-life is sticky; it rains nuclear showers
against all of our twisted, crooked, creaking shoulders.
    leila has claws. and fangs.
    leila is something fierce.
    <inescapable.>
    she is darkness, from the tips of her eyelashes to
the jagged, ragged edges of her pinky toenails.
    she is a shadow. a cipher. she is the opposite of
matter.
    she is ready.

    leila is chaos.

    we are *all*—

junior
shelly
leila
me—

we are all
<here>
<now>
<fierce deep inescapable>
<chaos>.

we are all driven by the undertow.

leila sits beside junior in the front seat of the car,
her head, as ever, tilted toward him, their collective
consciousness emitting
    <static.>
    <interference.>
    <white noise.>

on her lap she holds a sack,
once pristine white,
now frayed and filthy.
full.

shelly bounces beside me in the backseat, eyes
round and wide, humming, thrumming, vibrating. she is
tuned out, tuned *in* to leila and junior, to the crackling,
crashing sounds that call to us from the front of the car.

"it's time," junior explains, from behind the
steering wheel.
"Henry says: it's time."

junior is:
rudderless.
but.
junior is:
driven.
and i am:
carried along.
upswept.
adrift.
alone.
alongside
my family.

clatters and clangs emerge from leila's bag as our
car barrels down the road, away from death valley,
moving steadily along toward the canyons, the
fissures, the
<fault lines>

of the city of angels.

neophyte

i am hanging laundry to dry on the line when Henry
approaches me.

    laundry is one of my favorite chores on the ranch;
something about the casual baptism of fabrics, of the
sensation of suds, filmy and slick, and the clouds of filth
that collect in the wash basin.

    something about scrubbing,
    starting fresh.
    each time.
    i like to make things clean.

    but Henry has another task in mind for me, one
i wouldn't have thought myself ready for. He has
handpicked me,
    sees something worthy,
    deserving.
    in *me*.

    "we've got ourselves a newbie coming today," He
says. His voice is a crawl, a drawl that reaches for me,
snakes around my shoulders and down my throat like
honey, or cough syrup, like some type of heavy, heady
medicine.

    some kind of semitoxic magic.
    a *newbie*. another member of our family. because

Henry's love is overflowing, and there is always room
for someone new, for *more*.

because our family is a chain of paper dolls that
stretches past the edge of the
horizon.

"once you finish hanging the wash, why don't you
come on down to the general store? emmett could use
some company, anyway, while you wait."

i ask:
"leila?"

what i mean is:
where is leila?
leila likes to be in charge.

and also:
emmett belongs to leila.

"leila's taking care of her own stuff today."
Henry sets a hand on my shoulder so that my edges
blur.
i melt, ever so slightly.

"okay," i say.
"okay."

chemistry

emmett is asleep.

    when i arrive at the mouth of the ranch, at the
general store, my fingers wrinkled, puckered, smelling
of soap, emmett is pitched backward in his rocker on
the porch, straw hat lowered over his eyes, mouth slack.
a slight snore escapes from his chest at irregular beats.

    Henry winks at me like we are co-conspirators.

    "he'll never even miss her."

leila, He means.

emmett will never even know that leila was gone.

"perfect timing for your promotion."

promotion.

    there is a swell, a tidal wave that begins in my toes
and quickly gathers force.

promotion.

    i want to swoon.

    Henry glances at His watch. "she'll be here soon
enough."

    the *newbie*, that is.

    He looks at me.

    "time enough for a smoke.

what do you think?"

a *smoke*.
magic. tidal waves that swell,
that swoon.

i think:
<*yes of course always*>

i think:
a *smoke* is the one thing, the only thing,
    that could possibly make this moment sharper,
clearer. more crystallized.
    a smoke is the one thing that could make me burn
brighter,
        make me pop
        like a bottle rocket
        or a supernova
        lighting up the atmosphere,
        throwing sparks.

    that chemical undertow is the only sensation that
could ever begin to approach the high that i feel here,
on the ranch, swathed in ersatz-everything,
        singled out by Henry as the one.
        as *chosen*.
        even if it is only temporary,
        fleeting,
        ephemeral—

even if it is only for today.
today,
i am chosen.

i nod, as He knew i would, and watch as He disappears
two fingers into His back jeans pocket, a magician
coming to the end of a trick, fishes out a wad of tissue-
thin papers and a plastic baggie filled with fairy dust.
He pinches the fairy dust into a thick, plush line,
rolls the paper tightly. twists the ends together, seals
them between His lips.
lights the stick.
passes it to me.

i breathe.

in.
and out.
in.
and out.

i breathe.

in.
and out.

and float

away.

angel

the new girl is an angel.

    this is what i first think, when i scan her driver's license:

    angel.

    my head is, by now, saturated, *smoky*; a nest of cotton batting, a pleasantly dull anti-atmosphere of negatively charged ions.

    i watch as the girl, the *newbie*, lopes in slow, leggy strides toward the front steps of the general store, streaks of sunlight bouncing off of her shoulders as they shift in oiled ellipses.

    i think:
    angel.

    i don't realize that i've said the word aloud until she corrects me,

    coughs, hides her rosebud lips behind a graceful fist.

    "angel-*a*. rhodes."

    oh.
    i flush.
    of course.
    still. it was an honest
    mistake.

angel-*a* rhodes has piles of sun-colored ringlets
arranged in a halo
that twists around the crown of her head.
her eyes shimmer. her skirt is diaphanous, white
and gauzy
like the inside of my head.
it brushes the tips of her sandals
like a choirgirl's robe.
it was an honest
mistake.

"angel-*a* rhodes." i enunciate, clip my words sharply
now. her driver's license says that she is nineteen, and that
she has come to us from the far east—new hampshire.
    which only goes to show how expansive Henry's
orbit, His half-life—
how vast it truly is.

"i, uh—"
my mouth is suddenly filled with sand,
my head cloudier yet with
white noise,
interference. it is a play,
a performance,
and i have somehow forgotten
my lines.

i think back desperately to my own
arrival,

to leila and her lockbox.
to her angles and edges.

no.
even with a *promotion*, even having been *chosen*,
that could never be me.
i am not leila.
i have no angles, no edges.
no teeth.

i am only hollowed-out spaces.
i am only the opposite of matter.

i may be chosen—
today, i may be Henry's.
chosen.
but i am not,
will never be
leila.

rescue

shelly comes to my rescue.
    Henry must have told her, must have tipped her off,
    warned her that i might need a hand here, flailing,
that i might need some backup. support.
    and who better to offer that than my shadow-self?
    my *sister*?

    she rushes up behind me, arms outstretched. skirts
past me. squeezes angela so tightly that my own frame
constricts in sympathy.

    with a jolt, i recall when shelly first embraced me
that way. can still trace the outline of her lungs against
my own.
    the memory, the image, is just the jump start
that i need. it cuts through the cotton wool of Henry's
chemical undertow.
    my sister, shelly, always knows just what it is that i
need.
    i stand up straighter, roll my shoulders back
until my sight line is square with the supposition that
radiates from angela's steady, knowing gaze. i hold a
hand out for the rest of her personal effects.
    i imagine that i am leila:
    dream myself sharp teeth, angles,
    edges.

f a m i l y

angela is still.
"you know?" she offers, eyeing me casually,
"i think i'll hang on to this stuff. just for now."

it is not a question. not even a challenge.
it is simply a fact.

i swallow.
i know what leila would say to that:
everything stays here.

she'd rap her knuckles against the tinny frame of
the lockbox, and angel-*a* would genuflect.
leila would bare her teeth, and angela would
collapse in on herself like a dying star.

leila knows:
people's dirty secrets.
how best to make them bleed.
leila *knows.*

but.
i am not
leila.

so.
i swallow.
i blink.

i speculate
inwardly
as to what Henry might say about this
exchange.

but.
i don't say

anything

at all.

full

the campfire burns for angela.

she has just finished her first dinner with us, with
our *family*; now, we loll, sated and content, bathed and
backlit by the campfire's glowing embers.

i watched angela while she ate—
couldn't not-watch—
studied the twitches and quivers of her muscles,
the curves of her frame.

she isn't like the other sisters.

unlike the rest of us, angela didn't devour her
meal, didn't disappear into it. didn't consume it with
voracious need, with bottomless, infinite *want*. didn't
scrape her fork against her empty dish to capture every
last drop of sustenance, or lick the tracks the fork tines
left behind.

angela chewed thoughtfully. toyed with her
silverware. pushed her bowl aside when she'd eaten to
her fill.

said, *no, thank you*, when Henry dipped into His
ever-present bag of family medicine, of fairy dust.

until angela arrived, i don't think i'd realized that
there was such a thing as one's *fill*. hadn't known there
was such a thing as saying *no*

to Henry.

i would never want to say *no*
to Henry.

i am never
full.

i spied leila, across the leaping, dancing, dangerous
flames. i saw that she, too, had taken note of the limits
of angela's
appetites.
leila clicked her tongue against the back of her
teeth;
she all but *bared* her teeth.

angela may be
full.

but leila is
consumed.

welcome

there is a second part to my *promotion*.

 i have a second, separate job—a task, a responsibility to oversee in order to fully welcome angela into the fold.

 i have my orders.

 Henry explained it all to me back when we waited on the porch of the general store, back when i was wrapped in a blanket of heady, smoke-driven dreams of consciousness and anticipation.

 back when i basked in the beacon of being *chosen*.

 chosen. as i am:

 still. now.

 always.

 i have a task.

 over the lapping fire, the snaking, creeping smoke, i catch shelly's eye. she giggles, winks. squeezes at my shoulder with tight, warm fingers. presses her hands against the flesh of her thighs, pulls herself to her feet. tugs at my own clasped hands and pulls me up.

 arms hooked around the hollow curves of each other's waists, we slink in tandem along the circumference of the campfire, wander toward where angela is perched.

 Henry sits cross-legged atop the nearby picnic table. catches our eye. nods.

shelly and i light down on either side of angela.
shelly hooks a slender arm around the soft space
between angela's waistband and her top, rests her
nimble fingers on a hip.
    sighs.

    angela glances up, her face a question mark.
    tilts her halo at me, quizzical.

    i breathe:
in.
out.
in.

    this is my *now*, my moment to serve my family. this
is the task for which i have been
    chosen.
    this is my chance. to fulfill my orders.
    but.

    i freeze.
    shelly's musical laugh echoes in my ears, and:
    i freeze.

    i cannot speak, cannot so much as shift where i sit.
    i am cement-set.

    and angela's face is still a textbook
    waiting,

family

wanting,
to be read.

i shut my eyes, reach inside, clutch desperately at
the rule book that
<—*please oh please*—>
surely must reside at the base of my core.
i grapple helplessly for the lessons i have heard
Henry preach, for the infinite catechism that has
saturated my every cell.

but.
my splayed fingers come up empty:
words and gestures, directives, imperatives, all of
Henry's teachings—
they slither through my webbed spaces,
the open places of my self.
my splayed fingers come up empty.
i am
empty.

i look up, shake my head in the hopes of clearing
my thoughts.
i see shelly, my *sister*, gazing at me. her lips are
pursed, unsure. i open my mouth to implore her—
to explain to her that i've somehow been *erased*,
somehow robbed of language—
but the words are mesh, meaningless; they dribble
down my throat, run silent, like hourglass sand.

i don't. know.
anything.

after a moment, there is rescue:
hot breath on the back of my neck.
there is energy:
form, and matter.
there is solidity.
there is everything i am not.

Henry.
He is everything.
He is a fever, throwing sparks.

He lowers Himself to the ground, His eyes refracting
light so that the air before me seems to dazzle,
seems to shimmer.
seems to waver like a membrane.
like possibility.

i breathe:
in.
and out.
again.

"thing is," He says, grinning easily at angela, "it's your
first night here. and newbies get the royal treatment."

well.

could it be
that i am
jealous?
of my newfound
sister?

it could.
it could be.
it could very well
be.

angela is silent for a breath.
she bites her lower lip, draining it momentarily of
color. her eyes are narrow slits.
"um."

Henry's aura shines harder, telegraphs love and
light.
"why don't you head over to the barn with shelly
and mel?" He suggests, undeterred.
"they'll show you some familial love."
He is so close to her that they share a shadow, a
looming, shapeless, amalgamated figure
that creeps along the pebbled surface of the
ground.

"our family can be real friendly, i promise."

a promise. a *premise*.

and shelly and i are tasked with fulfilling it.
shelly and i are sworn to Henry.
to our *family*.

she is lucky, i venture. angela *is*. lucky.
i tickle the nape of her pale neck, twist an errant
curl around the length of my index finger.

i think:
when i was a newbie, i had junior to contend with.
junior and his cut-glass frame, his icy overcoating. his
bottomless *wants*.
whereas angela has shelly and me and soft mouths
and sisters and *always*.

she is new to our *family*.
and she is lucky.

i blink, feel the heat of the campfire along the
fragile edges of my eyelids.
i breathe in.
and out.

angela's face puckers. her eyes squint, and the
freckles that dot her cheeks contract and expand again.
she shakes her head, setting my probing finger
loose.

she breathes.

in.
and out.

she says:
"no, thank you."

no.
thank you.

there is a hiccup in my ears, in my chest, through
my spine. a ripple in the atmosphere that surrounds me.
there is no such thing as saying *no* to Henry.
no reason why anyone would want to.

i swoon. i sway.

shelly is rocked by the motion of my frame,
gathers me,
guides me away,
off to bed.

there is no collective familial embrace, no initiation
for our newcomer.
there is only shelly.

she cocoons me, swathes me, consumes me.
doesn't speak.
i don't speak, either.
i sleep.

i dream.

i breathe:
in.
and out.

in my mind,
i say *yes* to Henry.

now.
always.
infinitely.
yes.

gone

when i wake in the morning, angela is gone.
    she has left no trace, no track.
    no indication that she ever existed to begin with.

    with her, my first *promotion*, my first task—
my first failure at the hands of Henry—
disappears.

    it is a relief.

    we don't speak of her. none of us do.
certainly not Henry.

    it is as though she were a mirage. a fun-house
mirror-image.
    a collective hallucination.

    a cautionary tale.

immaculate

today, we are told to clean.
    today, Henry says, the ranch must be in pristine condition. immaculate.
    He is expecting a visitor.

    not another would-be sister, another shameless, empty imposter. another angela. nothing like that.
    angela does not exist for us, for our *family*, anymore. she is a wisp, a whisper, a faint outline that fades against each rainfall.
    it is almost as though she never existed at all.

    today, Henry is expecting someone
    <blank and>
    important.
    the music man who will widen our scope, our reach. our orbit.
    someone who can pull strings, can make things happen. someone who knows how to spread Henry's music, Henry's word.
    Henry's love.
    someone who will send Henry's message out and into the world, where it belongs. where it can be shared by all who seek joy. truth.
    love.
    <terror.>

someone who believes. who trusts.

someone who will widen our circle, burst the half-
life open.

someone who will ionize our ironbound orbit.

someone to multiply the sticky netting of our
family

exponentially.

it is time.

ties

still. i have to wonder. how Henry made His
connections.
  His ties.
  i understand, of course: His truth. His totality.
the trail that He leaves with anyone that He deigns to
touch.
  just the shadow, the suggestion, the outline of
Henry's being is enough; He links people, bonds them,
binds them irreversibly.
  He *is.* our pied piper.
  this, i know.

  but still, i have to wonder.
  about
  <*blank importance*>
  the visitor.
  about the man who, we are told, wants to spread
Henry's word. His message.
  His *love*.

  the ranch, as ever, is a disconnect. the ranch is
neverland,
  an imaginary playground.
  our family is self-contained.
  sequestered.

we have no windows,
looking out or in.

so how, then, does the visitor see us?
how did he find us?
where is Henry's point of origin?
where does His orbit
begin?

and how far
<how tightly>
do his ties
bind
?

la-la land

Henry says that the city of angels is, in fact, full of phonies.

He says it brims with half-truths and doublespeak, bursts with sleek, snakelike parasites, crawls with yawning, searching, devouring mouths looking to bleed you dry. to swallow you whole.

looking to *consume* you.

los angeles is dirty, a house of cards coated in a thin veneer of pixie dust. a place where magic is mere trickery, and

<hollow, ersatz>

"love" comes

<free>

cheap.

regardless, it is the most logical starting point for Him, for Henry:

los angeles.

it is a mecca, a point of origin for those who bear a message. it is littered with blank, important people who can make things happen.

if only they were people you could trust.

los angeles is filled with broken promises, unfulfilled premises, ersatz-everything. charlatans,

hucksters, tricksters. folks looking for a fast break, an
easy buck, an open door.
    an *in*.

    "whereas i," Henry says,
    "have always been

    out."

horizon

i don't believe it, really. not quite.

    i don't, won't, *cannot* fathom this notion, this ugly, aching whisper of a half-life.

    this idea of Henry ever being *out*, that is.

    the suggestion of Henry ever being pushed aside; being cast
    <far farther farthest>
away; being shuttled; swept off; shifted toward just beyond the endless, ageless, boundless horizon. being sent, spiraling, toward just past the limits of a collective, collapsing sight line.

    Henry is everything, after all.

    and *everything* is the opposite of *out*.

    but Henry says so. says that *it is so*. tells us how, time and again—

    how, *infinitely*—

He has been ushered to the wayside, carried to the outskirts, expelled. taken swiftly to the rough, rudderless edges of the undertow.

    <out.>

    He understands our doubt, our disbelief, of course. our flawless, blinding, boundless faith in Him, in His eternity.

but. He reminds us:

this is how He first found us, after all. first came upon us. first understood us.

first *saw* us. first *knew*.

us.

each of us. all of us.

this

<out>

outside, this undertow—this is how He sharpened His consciousness, His perception, His *now*.

His

<always>

orbit.

this is how He honed His pinprick-precise, razor-edged gaze. how He learned to best reflect the core, the coiled, curdled chasm of our inner mirror-selves.

how He uncovered our wants. how He collected us. how He gathered all of the

<broken>

wandering, wondering bodies, the drifting, shiftless members of our ever-growing

<family>

group.

this is where the recognition, the *yes*, *now*, *always* began.

this space, this in-between place—

this tangled tip of our universe's boundaries,

the horizon,

the craggy, quivering gap
just beyond the limits of our vision—
this is the point of origin.
this is where the orbit spun into being, where the
ions charged to life. how the shimmering, yawning
vortex began its
    <simmering smothering suffocating>
    deep, fierce, inescapable
    outward spiral.

so Henry says. to us. it is how He explains. how He
gathers us back, pulls us away from the thorny, knotted
edges of any ankle-deep doubt. from the muck, the rot,
the mire.
    it is how He herds us back toward His circle, back
into His consciousness. back toward the sanctum of His
orbit, His *always*, His infinite, ever-outward spiral.

and Henry's orbit—
His half-life, His atmosphere—
His *word*.
is.
always.
<infinity infinitely endless>
truth. peace.

love.

open

i open myself to Him,
      toward Him.
      to Henry.
      for Henry.
      still.
      now.
      always.

      at night,
      each night,
      when He will have me:
      i offer my hollow places.

      i still don't quite believe Him,
      still am not wholly convinced of the rejection
      He so casually references,
      of His
      <*word message truth*>
      preaching,
      His detailing of a
      feeble,
      fractured
      conscience.

      of blurred but binding boundaries, of a life—
      His life, sometime in the unspoken before—

on the outside, the outskirts.

after all,
there is no *outside of*—
can be no *alternative to*—
this space,
this collective sphere,
that
<*i we the family*>
we all
have come to know
as Henry's atmosphere.
His half-life.
His infinite
now.

so.
i open myself.
unfold.
for Him.
toward Him.
always
Him.
Henry.

i expose the howling, hollow places,
offer up the gentle, raw,
in-between spaces.
i listen for sounds.

<*always.*>
His sounds.
His word.
His music.
His
<*need?*>
His love.

i listen.
for Him.
and He comes to me.

gathered

i am not alone, of course.

    my folds and fissures are not the only hollows, the only fault lines that Henry knows.

    i am never alone with Henry, not since He first found me, first came upon me, crumpled, crouched, pulling back. first saw me cringing, collapsing inward. since He first recognized that i was
    <*nothing*>
little more than antimatter, a supernova amidst disintegration, imploding, unfurling, giving way to an ever-deepening black hole.
    giving way to despair.

    there is no *alone* on the ranch.
    on the ranch, life is full to bursting. life on the ranch overflows.
    life on the ranch is *everyone, always, now*.

    we may all have been ignored, abandoned, rejected by the
    <*not before no before never before*>
    blank, important visitor,
    but we still have our
    <*ties*>
    truth.

our love.
our center.
our rudder.
our
<undertow>
Henry.

we are
conjoined,
ephemeral,
infinite.
gathered.
waiting, awaiting:
more message,
more truth.
more love.
His love.

we are
<dirty hippies>
family.

patient

we are patient.
    gathered.
    we awaken,
    we await.
    we are quiet, clustered.
    bathed in shadow and smoke.
    swathed in starlight.
    biding our time.
    expectant.

    Henry has a message,
    a truth.
    a measure of love to dole out,
    to deliver.
    and we
    are

    open.

ego

the visitor has not arrived.

    the
    <blank and>
    important music man
    that Henry hopes will spread
    <His>
    our message—
    the *family's* message—

    he has not been by to tour our tattered, winding
wonderland. to take in, to drink down our collective,
fractured fantasy
    in our ersatz-everything ranch.

    no one has come
    to see us.
    to hear us.
    to hear *Him.*
    to listen
    to Henry's
    word.
    to revel in His
    love.

    on the first day, Henry awaits, ever hopeful, ever

aware. perches on the stoop of the general store, drums
graceful fingers against worn-in jeans.

smiles.

knows.

everything.

every secret tucked within every hollow space.

on the first day, the ranch is still immaculate.

pristine.

gleaming with promise

and anticipation.

Henry says:

there is no *i*, no *ego.*

Henry teaches that all we need is us:

our *family.*

but by the third day of waiting, His grin falters at
the corners.

by the third day without our visitor,

without a promise of a higher calling,

a platform, Henry's forehead

is a road map of worry.

Henry's lips purse together with an expression
so foreign to Him that at first, i hardly recognize the
emotion:

concern.

and by the third day, high desert winds have

kicked a fine coating of dust over the surface of our
surroundings
    so that we are no longer
    clean.

whispers

cocooned within a threadbare sheet
    flanked by *family*
    i inhale
    breathe in starlight,
    charged particles,
    antimatter
    and choke back
    doubt.

    through the thin layer of fabric that
    swaddles me,
    shelly's ribs expand
    and contract,
    press against my own.

    she sleeps soundly,
    her rhythms,
    her pulse, smooth,
    safe.

    all of our sisters—
    tucked tightly into warm, worn nests—
    sleep soundly.
    smooth.
    safe.

family

while i:
inhale.
breathe in dusk,
studs of starlight
antimatter
and choke back
doubt.

alone
amidst my family,
breathing my own ragged staccato,
i listen for sounds.
whispers.

they come to me,
unbidden.

once the campfire has been snuffed,
once Henry has chosen
and our family—
all of our fractured, shrieking bodies—
have been tucked tightly,
nestled into
worn, warm linens—

that is the hour
when the sounds come to me,
unbidden.
when the truth

seeps.
slithers.
wraps itself around my ankles
like seaweed,
rotted,
washed up at the water's edge
by the force of the roiling tide.

as i skate the knife-edge
between conscious and sleep,
between wake and trance,
between
worry and
safety,
a truth floats to the surface.
it dances like a whisper.
like a secret.
like a code.

at night,
when our barn is shadowed
in lace patterns of moonlight,
junior and leila
speak in code.

they perch on the covered porch
just outside our sleeping quarters.
they think
we are—

f
a
m
i
l
y

all of us—
asleep.

but
i can hear
the
whispers.

streaked,
split open
by the empty creak
of a shaky, spindly rocker—
i can hear the whispers,
their whispers,
all too well.

the secret goes:

leila and junior:
they worry.
about Henry's message,
His word.
they fear the music man
has forsaken us,
leaving us precious few ways
to peddle, to spread
to *deliver*
our word,
our prayer,

our gospel,
into the world.

leila sighs.
the squeak of her chair is a protest.
she says,
"Henry's getting restless."

restless.
the word sizzles on her tongue.

"wouldn't you be?" junior asks. "that man was
supposed to come. supposed to listen. to make a
recording of Henry's music."
  a beat, a pause, in which i imagine tented fingers,
a reflective gaze into the inky, empty darkness.
  (so familiar are the outlines of junior's body, his
boundaries, to me by now.)
  "money from the music would've gone a long way."
  the tapping of a work boot against a buckled,
softened wooden slat. the sound of force and friction,
of solid things, set to spoil.
  "money would've meant we could stop dealing. or
maybe, that we could stay here at the ranch forever."

  i can't see leila's face, of course,
  beyond the image unspooling
  in my mind's eye
  <familiar>,

but the hitch,
the moment, is
deadly.
potent.

"it's not about the money," she says, and her voice is
tight.
"it's about Henry's message."

junior chuckles, a rattling sound.
"yeah, and you think that's gonna pay our way
around here? you think emmett's just gonna give us a
free ride forever?"
his laugh is the cranking of a windup toy.

<dirty hippies.>
<no such thing as free love.>

"fine," leila says. her voice is clipped. "fair enough.
but:
Henry is as close to god
as anything i've ever known.
He *is*.
so:
it's not about money;
it's about the *message*.
the *word*.
the *truth*."

"it's about making all those people take notice,"
junior says, his windup-toy laugh turning over in the
midnight air.
  it sounds like maybe he is agreeing with leila.
  but maybe he is saying something else entirely.
  something *more*.
  something different.
  something dangerous.

  maybe it is—
  money.
  maybe it *is*,
  truly,
  music.
  or maybe it is,
  even—
  still,
  yet,
  love.

  pure
  and
  bright:
  love.

  maybe.

  but whatever

the cause
the catalyst
<*no ego no i*>
Henry cannot be
cast
aside.

whispers leak and trickle,
creeping toward me.
there is a tidal shift
slowly gathering force.
swift, almost imperceptible.
it rides,
it weaves,
it stings and burrows,
salt water, seaweed,
and other sunken things.

i hear the rush, the shower
within the parentheses—
the negative spaces—
of junior's and leila's
whispers.

there is no such thing as
free love.
there is no denying Henry.

and when we gather force,

knit together—
fuse—
there will be no
ignoring
our
family.

helter-skelter

a week passes.
     another dust storm, another campfire.
     whispers, creeping.
     engines kicking on,
     turning over.
     arrivals, exchanges
     secrets and dealings and fury and tides.

     but still
     no
     <blank>
     important
     visitor.

     another night with my sisters,
     my father,
     my *family*:
     more smoke,
     more medicine.
     more chemical summoning
     of the high tide.

     Henry exhales slowly, leans forward.
     presses His palms firmly to His knees.
     it is time for more truth,
     fireside wisdom.

time for us all—
for our *family*—
to
<*come to now*>
arise.

Henry has something to say.
a message to deliver.
some truth,
love,
wisdom
<*terror*>
to impart.

He starts:
"the man has tried
to keep me
down."

flame leaps,
laps at his ankles;
smoke drapes,
snakes,
swoons.
swaddles him in murky gray
haze.

a veil has dropped;
i see the outside world in fragments,

through spools of cotton batting
that muffle,
that cloak.

the man?
no, it's more than that.
more than the one visitor.

it is *all* of the
blank,
nameless,
faceless
men.

all of the uncles
creeping,
lurking
late at night.

filling up any open spaces
they can
find.

i hear Henry's message.
His word.
His truth.

i can relate.

men are:
sharp teeth,
slick canines.
bloodlust,
anger,
hunger.
empty spaces.
hollowed-out husks.
<uncles and elbows and knees pinned apart>

i can relate. i have been there.
i have been
<held down filled up choked off>.

but.
Henry was meant to erase all of that.
the premise of Henry—
His promise, His power—
was to wave a wand,
to wiggle a finger, to grant a wish
and make the *before* vanish,
dissolve,
desist.
to make me whole again.

instead,
there is the creep,
the seeping sting

of salt water
droplets, like tears,
clinging to the whispered words
passed between my *family*
in secret.
and the smoke
can only do
so much.
i breathe in what i can.
swallow it down
like a
whisper.

Henry catches my eye.
notes the heavy rise of my chest.
sees me.
sees *through* me.
knows.
everything.

He can taste the doubt i carry,
i think.
can cut through the cotton wool
to where
the worry
lives.
can sense my fear
of the building
undertow.

i breathe quickly, my heartbeat catching in my
throat,
to think that Henry so easily reads every secret
space of mine.
breathing brings the cloud-shifts back,
the lazy haze,
erases all traces of
<never>.
drowns me.
again.

i think:
Henry, too—
Henry, *Himself*—
has been suppressed.
has been swallowed,
consumed,
devoured.
considered and rejected
by this so-called
<man>.
this blank, important person
who is somehow *more*,
somehow infinite.
somehow *never*.
to think that Henry has bled.

<as though. as though there is were ever could be—
anything, anyone, any possibility of—more than Henry.>

guilt and anger wash over me, a sheen of
indignation,
    as the medicine takes hold.
    Henry.
    has been left. out.
    by this person, this
    <*charlatan huckster trickster*>
    visitor, who did not visit.
    who is little more than an unfulfilled premise.
    a broken promise. an execution of a plot.
    sinister. chaotic.
    potent
    and poised to strike.

    "the man didn't want me—didn't want any of *you*."

    the man. Henry means
    something larger than merely the stranger,
    the connections He thought were finally, fully
fusing.
    He means *everyone*,
    everything,
    infinity.

    we nod,
    collectively,
    contemplatively.
    we are rapt,

captive pupils.
we are devout disciples.
we are deadly intent.

no one can hurt
<*our family*>
Henry.

    a mumble, a moan, a barely contained squeal of
agreement escapes from leila's lips.
    she senses what must be done.
    the rest of us remain in silent agreement. we
know, too:
    Henry must not be kept down, suppressed,
silenced.
    Henry's love must not be restrained.
    Henry's word is truth.
    <*in Henry, we trust.*>
    we will deliver the message. His message.
    His word. His *never*.
    His *now*.

He says:
"the man has tried. to keep me down.

"but after armageddon—
after helter-skelter?
we're gonna show the man—

we're gonna show him how it's done.

"we are going to
<shriek fracture spiral out of orbit>

"rise."

arise

i do not know what helter-skelter is, what it is that
Henry means when He exhorts us to
    <rise>.

    but.

    i do know:
    that Henry—
    my father, my lover, my shadow-self—
    has been made to bleed.

    and i know:
    that my family protects one another.

    i know:
    another promise,
    however unspoken, has been forged.
    among us.
    in His name.
    among my *family*:

    we will
    <arise>.

clean

i have discovered:
    i like things clean.
    like the tidy/tidal order of the either/or.
    i like things neat,
    contained,
    filled in.

    so.
    i like to do the washing.
    of all the chores, the tasks—
    the banal, mundane,
    day-to-day delirium
    of my newfound, eternal *now*,
    of all the ways i'm given
    to pass the endless, *always*-time
    here in ersatz-everything—
    washing is the simplest.
    the most satisfying.
    soothing.
    we don't have a machine on the ranch,
    but i don't mind.

    i have discovered:
    i like things clean.

    we don't have a machine,

so instead, i wash by hand.
i use a low, wide aluminum tub that is kept out
behind the barn;
once a week, i fill it from a thick, waxy tangle
of green garden hose
and chalky, lumpy soap
that leila and shelly melt down
from salvaged scraps of store-bought bars.

the wash water is always cold,
always a slap,
a gasp,
a breathless shock that catches,
clenches
at the base of my stomach.
it grabs me deep,
takes me by surprise,
each time.
each time,
i plunge my hands into the icy suds
and contract,
instantly bracing against the
sharp awakening.
each time,
i fold in upon myself,
shrink at least nine sizes.

i reel.
each time.

but.
i always regain my footing quickly.
always recoil,
rebound.
the soapy slop is an alarm,
a siren,
a knife slipped smoothly
into the soft, hollow space
below my rib cage.
it rouses me.
methodically,
almost rhythmically, i rise,
step back.
begin the baptism.
again.
always.

i douse the articles of clothing,
one at a time,
lower them each in turn
into the shallow, murky pool,
watch them darken and swell
with saturation.
i press,
i knead,
i twist,
enjoying the sensation of frigid backsplash
against the goosefleshed surface of my
bare arms.

i have discovered:
i like to do the
washing.
the process is
an exercise in
zen.
clarity.
purity.
i like things
clean.

my favorite part is when i am finally finished,
when i've draped the clothes—
my *family's* clothes—
across the low-slung line to dry.
when i can step back, proud and tired,
squint,
see them sway in the sunlight
like hollowed-out ghosts,
like outlines.
like suggestions
of something *more*,
something whole.
something full.
supple.
something maybe
perfect.

i have even removed

most of the blood from that night.
from shelly's fever dream.
a slight stain remains,
a smudge,
a photo negative of what was lost.
some things can't be scrubbed out.
and shelly spends ever-increasing time on her own,
nestled,
motionless,
curled beneath new bedsheets,
contemplating something more.
something whole.
something full.
supple.
something maybe
perfect.
a slight stain remains.
some things can't be scrubbed out.

fever dreams aside,
we don't produce much washing.
the family. doesn't.
despite how full to bursting life on the ranch
can be.
   <dirty hippies.>
   leila and the other sisters would just as soon go
bare, natural,
   exposed
   <open>.

so that once a week, i am mostly sorting through
the pockets
of Henry, junior, and the other men
<dirty dealings?>
who come around.

sometimes, i find things. in the washing.
once a week, while sifting through the dirty laundry,
i find things. i come across all sorts of interesting
things,
while i do the washing.
you wouldn't believe the sorts of things that some
people waste.
the things that people sometimes throw away.

for example:
it is an overcast morning—
i don't know what day it is,
haven't known the day or date
since Henry first stumbled upon me back in the
haight
(we have no use for calendars, here at the ranch)—
but.
it is morning, because that is part of the routine,
my routine,
for laundry.
morning. is.

so.

it is morning,
and i am awake.
ready to begin the weekly baptism.
i shake out junior's pants legs,
reach inside his pockets to turn them inside out,
and a long, smooth, glossy object flies out of a
pocket and lands at my feet.
the object beckons like a jewel;
i have a flash of muddled recognition.
<?>

i bend at the waist, crouch down,
grab at it, run my fingers along cool steel grooves.
a knife.
a switchblade,
big, bigger
than any i've seen before.

the knife is scratched but sturdy,
solid against the flat face of my palm.
when i press against its release,
a swath of sharpened metal
kisses the thinnest part
of my skin.

i wonder, briefly,
what junior plans to use it for.
but of course, i can't ask.
will not ask.

of course, there is no *why*.
not here.
not ever.
so. i don't ask.
<*anything. ever.*>

i turn the blade again,
shudder to see its lengthy surface gleam.
it is big, bigger.
it is a threat.
and i am afraid.

i set the knife aside to be
returned.
and i worry.

later, after lunch, i track junior down.
i tug at his shirt,
reluctantly hand him back the knife,
push the thought of its cocked,
spring-loaded potency
to the far corners of my mind.
i tamp down the worry.
the fear.
the fray.

junior peers at the knife,
arches an eyebrow,
purses his lips.

smiles
with recognition.
"that ain't mine," he says, grinning.
"it's Henry's. i was just borrowing it.
Henry wanted me to get a feel for it,
to get ready for helter-skelter.

"it's Henry's," junior says.
"you can return it
to Him."

so
i do.

i return it—
the knife—
to Henry,
without another
word.
without a sound.
without question.

but not
without
<worry>,

not
without
the cold,

clenching shock
of
slowly growing
fear.

not
without
wondering
<*why?*>
still.

worry

it has been thirteen days.
    thirteen days since we cleaned, since we made the
ranch
    <immaculate>.
    thirteen days since i
    first contemplated,
    first considered.
    first thought about
    connections
    <ties>.

    thirteen days since junior
    first let spill,
    first whispered to leila,
    first told the truth about
    Henry's savage past-life,
    His mirror-self,
    His muddy
    underside.
    His brushes with
    <violence chaos blood>
    <the man>
    <helter-skelter>
    the law.

    the story goes:

when Henry was still small,
still a boy,
His mother traded Him
for a pitcher of beer.
a pitcher.
of *beer*.
you wouldn't believe the sorts of things
that some people
throw away.

but.
there was *rescue*.
Henry had a savior:
a man. an uncle.
and Henry was rescued.

but.

when Henry's uncle returned Him to His mother,
she tossed Him right back out onto the street.
slapped Him straight back down onto the trash heap.
she didn't want motherhood.
didn't want a son.
didn't want Henry.

to hear junior tell it, Henry
<*arose*>
learned quickly, adapted,
realized how to take the things

that weren't on offer.
how to fend for Himself.
how to feed the yawning *want*.
how to fill in the cracks,
the fissures,
the rivulets.
the fault lines.

but.

i think:
He never did make Himself
whole again.

and *now*.
His connections, His *ties*—
they teem,
they twist,
they tangle.

and i worry:

that
they spoil.
they sour.
they shrink.
they fray.
they
decay.

and we,
the family:
we burn.
slowly.
silently.
but ever steadily.
we fracture
and
split
at the
seams.

i worry:

that
He cannot bind us,
can't piece us together,
keep us together.
can't ever make us
whole or perfect.

i worry:

that
this latest rejection is gravity,
a magnetic charge, pulling Henry down.
and that we are tumbling after Him.

that we are all

collapsing in on ourselves
like a collective dying star.

junior speaks of payback,
of making a point,
of making ourselves heard.

leila has ideas of
how to get the world's attention.
how to spark.
Henry's half-life has an orbit
that cannot be
contained.

i worry:

that
Henry cannot restrain His infinite *want*.
cannot still the undertow within.

that Henry
wants
to spread chaos—
violence and bloodlust—
in His name.

and that we
are all of us
drowning

<alone>

together.

thirteen days.
in a place where time is not assigned.
where hours and errands are
empty
and open.

thirteen days is enough time
to feel the slow, stinging drip,
the pinprick,
the heartbeat of a measured poison.
the promise, the premise,
of deadly intent.

thirteen days feels
<come to now>
eternal
when you
are starting
to
unravel.
to
fray.
and to feel

afraid.

blood

my sister, shelly, always knows just what it is that i need.

so:
when i worry, i seek her out.

she is. my *sister.*
and she always knows
just what it is i need.

she *knows*, shelly does—
how to quell the constant fear.

how to quiet the clawing fists of doubt.
how best to bind the fraying edges
of my shattered reflection.

her mouth is a song,
a prayer.
a promise

of what *infinity* means.
of *family.*

and so:
tonight,
i seek her out.

i search for her.

but she is not at dinner.

she is not at dinner, which is unlike shelly,
my *sister*,
my shadow-self of bottomless hunger,
of cavernous *wants*.
of infinite *needs*.

she is *missing*.
she is *gone*.
and i:
worry.

when others ask,
i play at casual.

i pretend to know just what exactly shelly is up to.
just where she could possibly be, if not busily
feeding the
<*yawning chasms*>
that i,
her sister,
know to be her empty places.
her hollow spaces.
that i know to be her half-life.

i play at casual.

i arrange a spoonful of rice in an artful heap in a
bowl. i tilt toward the campfire. i drink down the flame.
i balance a serving spoon on my hip.

"oh, shelly?" i ask,
nonchalance draped like a cloak
across my shoulders.

"she's fine.
she went to sleep early.
she's fine."

and yet:
a fist clenches forcefully
at the back of my throat.
the flesh of my arms prickles.

i toy with the word, with the smooth, cool syllable,
roll it on my tongue:
"fine."

shelly's bowl, the bowl i have fixed for my absent
sister,
is balanced against my jutting hip bone.
my eyes dart nervously.
i make my way to the last place i saw her:
the general store.
(but actually, that was quite a few hours ago.)

i worry.

i rap, apprehensive, on the splintering door frame.
no one approaches Henry's domain without
express invitation, of course.
i know this.
this, i know.
but i am worried.

a beat.
only the sound of my insides,
the rhythm of my blood in my veins
to soothe me.

i breathe:
in.
and out.

the door swings open.

junior peeks out, his forehead sagging, his eyes
vacant.
"mel," he says. "come in."

so i do.

i step past him, breathe in. shrug my shoulders,
draw my aura

up about my collarbones. straighten my spine,
harden my imagined outer shell.

"i was looking for shelly." i thrust the bowl toward
him.
he takes it in, gaze flickering. doesn't take it.
instead just points for me
to set it down on a warped, uneven shelf.
so i do.

junior nods shortly, curves a hand around my elbow.
leads me gently
<gentle people>
toward a fringed silk curtain.

as i pass, i spot
the metal lockbox where leila keeps our valuables.
propped open, yawning,
coins, cards, trinkets, strewn.
and perched atop
a shriveled clump of dirty dollar bills
<no such thing as free love>
a scrap of paper
covered in scratchy scrawl.

but before i can wonder
<a promise?>
<a premise?>
<a deadly threat?>

i am ushered behind the curtain
and the veil is
lifted.

i blink.
i catch.
i swoon.
i sway.

junior braces me, bolsters me against his frame,
his arm cold and solid,
    like mechanics.
    like the undertow.

i breathe.

the blood is everywhere.
the air smells of copper and cloying.
the blood. *is.*
everywhere.

i spot a mattress on the floor;
the same space where Henry and i so often fuse
our fires,
    so readily collapse our hollow places.
    so readily devour each other.
    so eagerly swallow each other whole.

a jumble of sheets are clustered in a tangle,

soaked with sweat and blood.

shelly lies atop the mattress, splayed, struggling.
soaked with sweat and blood.

everything inside me screams.

she is my *sister*.
she is my shadow-self.

and she is
broken.
bleeding.

i rush to her side, kneel next to her.
fight against the roiling bile.

no matter:
she is lost to a fever dream.

i offer her a kiss on the forehead.
inhale the sheen of her sweat
as her body throws sparks.

junior leads me back outside,
back to where
cool air kisses
my slick flesh.

"she lost the baby," he says,
as deep inside of my core, a
hair trigger releases.

"she lost the baby," he says again,
softer,

"but

"she'll be okay."

lost

a beat.

    i breathe:
    in.
    and out.

    i reel.
    i retch.
    my hollow places clench.

    but unlike shelly,
    i am *fine*, truly.
    surely not soaked in blood,
    not slick with bright, loud pain.
    no.

    not like shelly. my sister.

    unlike shelly,
    my own fever dream is imagined,
    ersatz.
    my own flesh is cool to the touch.

    unlike shelly,
    my own bones are sheer,
    sheet-glass icicles.

micol ostow

my pulse pounds,
and sturdy fingertips close across
my shoulders:
Henry.

the force of his touch upends me,
sends me staggering.
i stumble to my knees.
force back a sob. choke.

"she's going to be fine," He says.
"this wasn't the time."

wasn't the time?
to grow our family?
i swallow.

and here i had
always thought
our time
as a family
was

infinite.

serious

Henry can read the fault lines of my face, of course.
of course He can.
He sees the fragile fragments of my sheet-glass
skeleton as they crumble,
as they collapse.
hears the shriek as the sand runs down the
hourglass tunnel.

"motherhood is serious business," He says,
like this is something i don't know about.

like i have no mother,
just the
looming vortex
that once swallowed mirror-mel whole.
like He, Henry,
is the beginning and end
of my *family*.

"we have lots of babies on the ranch," i remind Him,
feeling the round, full words
fill up my mouth,
taste the sour tinge of
protest.

"true."

He twists a strand of my hair around
His fist.
tenderly, at first.

and then:
my neck snaps back as He tugs,
pulls tightly.
it doesn't hurt,
not exactly.
but.

"if shelly wasn't ready to tell us about the baby,"
He continues, His voice low,
"then how could she be ready to bring a baby
into this
family?"

it occurs to me:
that there is one person that shelly did tell.
about the baby.
one *sister.*

and that:
if Henry knows that shelly
was keeping a secret?

well, then—
He might just know
that she wasn't

f
a
m
i
l
y

the only one.

well, then.

just like that,
the pressure on my scalp
is released
and my hair swings free,
forms a curtain around my shoulders.
shades the angles of my sunken cheekbones.
mutes my vision.
blurs things.

"i'm sorry," i say.

i am not sure for what,
but that is no matter.
i *am.* sorry.

Henry steps in front of me,
brushes my hair back again.
His fingertips graze my chin.

His eyes are satellites,
missiles,
moonbeams.
and i am drowning
again.

i *am*. sorry.
for so many things.

"mel," He whispers,
his lips vibrating against the pink of my ear,
"you know there's something coming."

i nod, slight, imperceptible.
think about the lockbox, the vortex,
scrap of paper written in code.
<helter–skelter.>

"and when it's time,
you're gonna have to do just exactly what junior
says."
<junior wants.>

His hands slip under the hem of my shirt, skirt the
surface of my skin.
send me swooning.
His mouth finds mine and we almost speak with
one tongue.
are almost one body.

"can you do that for me?"

i can't say if the question is spoken aloud,
or if it merely echoes in my head.

but that is no matter.

of course.
of *course*.
He is everything. He *is*. Henry.
and i
would do
anything
for
Him.

frayed

bars may bind,
      entwine,
      encase.
      encapsulate.
      and *the man*
      <*sharp teeth*>
      <*slick canines*>
      <*bloodlust*>
      <*chaos*>
      <*violence*>
      may have tried to keep Henry
      down.

      but.

      still,
      He managed
      to make,
      to forge,
      to foster
      <*ties*>
      connections.

      Henry brings people
      together.

family

<mostly. usually.>
He knits and weaves
<smothers and stifles>.

Henry has friends who are
<blank and>
important.
who want to spread
His love
<and terror>.

this is what He tells us.
when we gather.
when He preaches.
this is what we believe.

this is our truth,
our word.
our *always.*
Henry is love
<and terror>.

no one has come to visit.
no one has lighted down upon the ranch,
eager to spread the gospel of Henry's music.

it is a waste
<you wouldn't believe>.

Henry's ties are
<*ephemeral*>
frayed,
unraveling.
disentangling.

and i
worry.

it has been twenty days.

after

<helter-skelter.
    love and terror.
    the devil's business.
    sounds.>

    something fierce.
    somewhere deep.
    someplace inescapable.

spark

helter-skelter is coming.
    this is what Henry says.
    this is Henry's truth. His message. His gospel.
His
<terror>
love.

    "when it's time, you're gonna have to do just exactly
what junior says."

    "the man is in for a big surprise," Henry says.
    "you'll see."

    at night, when the rest of the family is
    nestled,
    resting, soundless,
    Henry rouses us,
    outlines
    how it will be.

    junior.
    shelly.
    leila.
    me.
    we are chosen

to bear His message.

we are precious.
and my doubt
easy enough to tamp down.
to drown.

we—
the outcast,
the abandoned,
the hapless,
the helpless—
the
< *dirty hippies* >
rejects,
the trash—
the *family.*
we.

we *will*:
rouse,
rise,
arise.
catalyze.
awaken.
we will set the end of days
in motion.

we will swell, swarm, spiral.

we will light the match to spark
infinity.

Henry's switchblade is a trigger,
a flint stone,
and when it is time,
we will ignite.

Henry's lips against my earlobe,
a whisper of divinity, of clarity:
"when it's time,
you're gonna have to do just exactly what junior says.
you're gonna have to be strong. swift.
you, *melinda—"*
<*me!*>
"you *are.* chosen."

<*i* am.>

"you *will be my messenger.*
you *will speak my words.*

"the man is in for a big surprise,"
Henry says.

"you'll see."

part III

now

1.
"it's time, mel. get dressed."

> my eyelids flutter.
> i struggle, briefly.
> thrash against the hour.
> strain to pierce the eggshell-thin,
> frail,
> fragile veil
> between conscious
> and light,
> between coma
> and wake.
>
> between
> *before*,
> *always*, and
> *never*.
>
> between *now* and *infinity*.
> between my half-life, heaven, and
> *<never not ever no such thing as>*
> hell.
>
> i have a stupefying moment of *who/where/how*,
> and then realize all at once, in a dizzying rush, a flood
> of *yes*.

oh. *yes.*
a barrage, a watershed of *come to now.*
i realize:

it is time.

2.
i cough, press my palms hard against the open-slatted
floor,
    feel the ridges, the grooves and indentations,
    feel so much past-life, history, so much *before*,
burrowed, carved deep beneath the surface.

    i wonder what i've left of myself here, forever
etched
    <burned>
    into the skeleton scaffolds of
    neverland.
    i marvel at the reach, at the radius of my
mirror-self, the eternity of just who i've become, the
endlessness of my
    newfound
    <family>
    ties.

3.
i stretch back from my mattress, rise.
　　my bones make a hollow,
　　creaking sound as i stand,
　　shaking off sleep,
　　slights,
　　shrugging out from beneath countless anonymous
　　insecurities,
　　wordless queries,
　　soundless questions.
　　shedding the skin of the mel behind the
　　looking glass,
　　the mel i was
　　<no i no ego>
　　<no not never>
　　before.

　　before i became everything that Henry promised.
　　before i burned. frayed.
　　feared.

　　before i unfurled,
　　opened myself,
　　offered up my hollow places,
　　exposed my smooth undersides,
　　my pliant insides.

　　before i bled.
　　for Him.

4.
the creaking, the pops and hiccups that sound as i rise,
they startle me.

they are the sounds of my skeleton snapping into
place, the sounds of my skin, bone, sinew,

settling.

of my pockets, my pieces, expanding and
contracting with my every

bated breath.

they are the sounds of my body reshaping itself,
readying itself.

reeling.

they are the sounds of the opposite of solid.

it is time.
it is late. it is the witching hour.
helter-skelter is upon us.
helter-skelter *is*
us.
the messengers.
the holy choir.
the harbingers of doom.

5.
junior's face hovers, inches from my own.

  i sense him, feel the edges of his skin
  ooze,
  radiate,
  pulsate with energy,
  with anticipation, with
  yes, *now*,
  always.

  junior *wants*.
  it is the type of *want* you could clutch, you could
grasp;
  the type of *want* you could wind around a crooked
finger.
  through the tar-thick, viscous cover of night, i
can feel it, the *want*, constricting across my shoulders,
weaving about my collarbones like a dusty noose.
  i can inhale and breathe his *want* into me so fiercely
that i can almost taste its rancor.
  can almost pretend it's my own.
  almost.

6.

it has been too long, here on the ranch. here in ersatz-
everything, here without windows, without edges,
without

<interference>

far too long.

so much so, *so* long, that it has begun to feel that
our *infinity*, our collective orbit, might be fading.

losing shape, strength, elasticity.

might be fraying. unfurling.

might be washing away like an etching in the sand
as the tide comes in

and slowly,

steadily—

but irreversibly—

erases what once was.

leaves only the *now*.

unwinds,

unravels infinity,

indefinitely.

i am not surprised to realize this.

after all, infinity has always felt impossible to me.

there is nothing, after all, that doesn't

end.

7.
it is here.
    <helter-skelter.>
    the *now,*
    everything that Henry has
    spoken of.
    it is tonight.

    tonight, we rise, and journey past the fault lines of
death valley. through the canyons and craggy terrain,
out toward where the blank, important people secure
themselves, squirrel themselves away.

    we—
    junior, leila, shelly, and
    <no ego no i>
    me,
    my half-life—
    my shattered, fractured, mirror-self—
    we have a message to deliver.
    His message. Henry's. of
    <love and>
    terror and torture and undertow.
    His reminder of what it feels like to drown.
    to be held down, filled up, choked off.
    of sharp teeth, slick canines.
    of bloodlust, anger, hunger.
    of empty spaces. of hollowed-out husks.
    of uncles and elbows and knees pinned apart.

of breathlessness. of afterlife.
of what it truly means to

come

to

now.

8.
we are fragile and fractured.

    we are family.

    we are fraying.

    but.

    rather than

    unravel.

    we will

    rise.

    we are poised to set the city of angels afire.

    we burn, we shrink, we shriek.

    we are coiled, potent, poison, ready to ignite.

    and Henry's message will be heard.

    now.

    always.

    tonight.

9.

He doesn't come with us, Henry.

He can't, shouldn't, won't; doesn't exist within our orbit, our shallow, washed atmosphere. He is our rudder, our tide, our current, but *now*, tonight:

we are the undertow.

we are messengers, harbingers, doomsday prophets.

we are *chosen*.

we are chaos, fierce and deep.

we are inescapable.

10.
we know what to do, what we must do,
    how exactly to go about setting the world
    ablaze.
    how to spark.

    "make it messy," Henry said. *"show the people what*
happens to their sons and daughters when they refuse to see
the now."

    He had an address, though not one i recognized, of
course.
    and of course, i don't ask questions.
    there is no *why*, no *before*, only this:
    blood. fear. chaos.
    power. poison.

    helter-skelter,
    and infinity,

    and mirror-mel,
    still trapped,
    pressed, soundless
    beneath the looking glass,
    its reflective surface a sheen, a sheath,
    a sheet of ice
    that separates:
    before and *after*
    broken and *whole*

fractured
but
patched,
patiently.
prepared for what is
now.

mirror-mel sees me,
signals to me
wordlessly;
she traces warning signals against the
frosted panes of her
transparent,
ever-present,
crystal coffin.
collapsing, gasping, drowning.
folding in upon herself.
afraid.

11.
i see her, mirror-mel—
　　see her at a distance,
　　as though she's a mere shadow,
　　just a fragment of my former self,
　　a cipher, an outline.
　　a whisper,
　　a wisp.
　　a suggestion.

　　mirror-mel does not bleed; when she weeps, her
face is a mask lit from the inside, streaked with sorrow,
stained with someone else's tears.
　　mirror-mel is a broken promise.

　　she is my *never*,
　　the jagged edge of my ruptured psyche,
　　my *me* that i have
　　<abandoned rejected cast out>
　　learned to do
　　without.

　　a frozen fragment of my
　　<not before no before never before>
　　unspeakable past.

　　but
　　even with
　　a chilly force field

a shield of charged ions
an icy screen the width of an ocean—
even still—
she and i,
we are conjoined,
ephemeral,
infinite.

we are paper dolls.

and i—
alone—
i:
am still, now,
<*always*>
broken.

12.
we have been chosen.

junior, shelly, leila, and i—
we, together, have been chosen,
anointed,
elevated.
handpicked by Henry to speak for Him.
to preach the word.
the truth.
the love.
the terror.

He bursts with love;
He overflows,
and we are vessels.
unique.
<blank and>
important.

we will preach the gospel;
foretell psalms of savage disarray.
we will tell tales of violence,
bloodlust.
chaos.

we are a choir of coiled fury,
of anger, of hunger.
a harmony of dissidence. .

we are sharp and slick.

Henry has prepared for us, for everyone—
for the *family*, for *infinity*—
He has prepared a
<*singer*>
sacrifice to be offered,
a gateway,
a talisman to incite,
ignite,
illuminate the pathway to the great
beyond.

we have purpose.
Henry's purpose.
we are poison.
we are fever.
we burn.

13.

junior and leila hurry, stuff supplies into a single filthy
sack, while shelly coats the planes and angles of her face
with heavy greasepaint.

i have only just changed clothing, just begun to
shroud myself in bleak, black cover when Henry appears
behind me, touches my shoulder lightly, ushers me
aside.

His gaze is a tunnel, a well, a portal to an
underground hideaway. mud and ink and danger churn
within His veins, swell and seep, leak from the scarred
surfaces of His skin.

i swoon. i crumple. i collapse inward on myself.

i am a dying star.

"listen, mel," He explains, "junior knows what to
do. you just follow him, go along with whatever he says."

i nod, thinking of heads tilted toward each other,
of whispers, of weapons tucked away. of gleaming knife
blades. of bright, swift pain. of the threat, of the dark-
edged promise that arises, rouses, roils within my co-
conspirators.

thinking of the chaos behind their eyes, beneath
the masks my sisters and my brother wear.

i know.

i know what *helter-skelter* means, what it is we're
meant to do for Him. for Henry.

the need, the now, the *want*:
it is that our message, our word, our *love*—
that it, that *we*, will set the world aflame.
that we will be the spark.
that we will remain, still, after,
when the tide rushes in again.
that we will be alone. together.
that we will be infinity.
that we will be *family*.
still.
after.
always.

Henry opens a palm; flat tablets wink back up at us.
four round, pressed promises of
fire, fuel,
of consciousness, of overdrive.
of chemical undertow, hunger, and need.
we swallow them down.

and as the pill
dissolves against my tongue,
mirror-mel—
her half-life,
her second thoughts
her silent doubts—
mirror-mel's unspoken
protests
dry up.

they crack and crumble like
a forgotten riverbed.

everything—
all of the *before*,
ever—
crumbles,
carried off.
forgotten.

and my mind
unfolds.
fueled by Henry's *want*.
His orbit.

for the moment—
in the moment—
my mind
my *self*
<*my spark*
takes hold>
unfolds.

14.

leila is dressed in black:

    black jeans, black boots, slim black turtleneck
pulled over her taut, slender frame.

    she is a spring-loaded coil, coated in ink. she is
slick, she is thick, she is heavy with sinister expectation.

    she is the execution of a plot, a plan.

    a threat.

    hollow need hangs from her.

    want drips from her limbs, caresses her joints,
pools within her crevasses, her cracks, her rivulets.

    she brims, bursts,

    overflows with *now.*

    her half-life is sticky; it rains nuclear showers
against all of our twisted, crooked,

    creaking shoulders.

    leila has claws. and fangs.

    leila is something fierce.

    <inescapable.>

    she is darkness, from the tips of her eyelashes to
the jagged, ragged edges of her pinky toenails.

    she is a shadow. a cipher. she is the opposite of
matter.

    she is ready. to creep. and crawl. but for real.

    leila is chaos.

    she is purpose.

    she is—

    <we are all*—junior. shelly. leila. me—>*

    we are *all—*

family

\<here\>
\<now\>
\<fierce deep inescapable\>
\<chaos\>
deadly intent.

we are all driven by the
undertow.

15.
leila sits beside junior in the front seat of the car,
her head, as ever, tilted toward him, their collective
consciousness emitting
> *<static.>*
> *<interference.>*
> *<white noise.>*

> i realize:
> even through the glitter of
> Henry's pills—
> His unspoken promise—
> their *spark* unsettles me
> fills the back of my throat like glue,
> like clay,
> like shards of broken glass.

> junior and leila
> are live wires.
> they *spark.*

> from beside me,
> shelly shines,
> radiates
> silently.

> while i:
> worry.
> i fear.

i unravel.

i swallow down sticky rivers of
fright
of doubt,
the buzz
<interference>
that wants to penetrate the hazy mask of
<magic medicine fairy dust fuel fire>
the undertow.
wants to rise above
the waterline.

but then,
again:
a wave.
again.

another hit,
a heady
heavy
rush
of chemistry
of infinity—
of
Henry's potion:

it seeps,
it creeps through narrow passageways,

neurons,
the fragile tubes and tissue,
the road map of my insides.

it soaks,
sinks claws into my deepest parts,
stains my skin from underneath,
beneath.

it takes hold.
electrifies me.

like a tidal wave

the undertow
overtakes me.

again.

16.
on leila's lap she holds a sack, once pristine white, now
frayed and filthy.

    full.

17.

shelly bounces beside me in the backseat, eyes round
and wide, humming, thrumming, vibrating. she is
tuned out, tuned *in* to leila and junior, to the crackling,
crashing sounds that call to us from the front of the car.

she unfurls, unfolds. opens.

shelly welcomes the static, the interference, the
rough, irregular edges of the horizon. she expands,
overflows. she showers me with her sense of tense
anticipation, her runny, formless awakening.

shelly is *so much.*
she. *is.*
so much.
too much.

and i am a vortex.
i am empty.

i am
the filmy
flimsy
threat
of slowly
unspooling
hesitation.

i am longing.
i am fear.

but still
even
yet
now:
underneath,
beneath,
i am guided by the riptide.
carried by the undertow.

adrift.

18.
clatters and clangs emerge from leila's bag as our car
barrels down the road, away from death valley, moving
steadily along toward the canyons, the fissures, the
    <fault lines>
    of the city of angels.

19.
the air inside our car is sour.
    it stinks of living things that have set to spoil; of acrid anti-energy, of cloud covers, impenetrable and dank.

    the air is fetid, and the surfaces around me are soaked,
    seeping with noxious, toxic filth.
    with waste.
    <trash>
    <you wouldn't believe>

    i take shallow breaths. my heart hammers. my *now* is playing at the wrong speed.

    i am doubt, afterthought. i am raw red nerve endings and cells misfiring, tissue and fluid and soft, yielding bone. pieces, pockets; parts that mesh, that mingle, that mix.

    i am a membrane that has been stretched, been tugged inside out, shredded to little more than thin, flimsy strings of silk.

    i have no boundaries.
    i have no limit.
    i have no horizon that i can see.
    i am exposed. soft. yielding.
    fluid.

i have been chosen.
handpicked.

and as our car is pulled,
guided by moonlight
and an unseen magnetic force,
the horizon slips
ever further
beyond my sight line.
beyond my ghostly grasp.

20.
we have:
      an address.
      a mission.
      a message.

      we have:
      a purpose.
      intent.

      we have:
      need
      want
      chaos.

      we have:
      our undertow.

      we have:
      now.

21.
there are gates.

>   where the
>   <*sacrifice*>
>   singer lives,
>   there are gates.

>   gates, and snarls of wires, flickering switchboards
that bind, that form a boundary.
>   she is contained. secure. squirreled away. her half-
life knows borders, knows the hard shell of safety.

>   but. our vortex? our *want*?
>   our *need*. has claws. and fangs.
>   and we have come to this night
>   <*to* now>,
>   prepared
>   to battle.

22.
junior cuts the telephone wire, steady, sure-handed.

   leila clips the chains around the front gate, feather-weight, aflight.

   shelly snips at cords, shorts the boxes, quiets the blinks and chirps that would otherwise sound our arrival. our arising.

   she cackles, rubs at the streaks of greasepaint on her face, grinds it into the hollows beneath her cheekbones. her eyes peer out at me from the carved expanse of her face, diamonds sunk deep within a pool of mud.

   i do not recognize my sister.
   my sister is an outline of her former self.

23.
outside of the car, the air is stagnant. the night is still.

    this house, this compound, lays tucked within the canyons of the pacific coast. the only sounds that drift our way are echoes, static transmitted from a distant plane, from a frequency far beyond our orbit.

    leila nods to herself.

    "perfect," she says.
    "this place is perfect."

24.
i look away, glance down at my feet, marvel mindlessly
at the contrast between the rubbed-out soles of my dull,
worn shoes and the sudden, sharp angles of the lush,
verdant lawn below.

the green grass is a cover, a casing. a boundary, a
slick, slippery shell. i want to crouch down, to grasp
each dew-soaked blade within my fault-lined palms, to
twist the silky strands against my twitching fingertips.

i wonder.

about the things beneath, i mean.
about the underneath.

about what could potentially lurk, crawl, slither
beneath the surface of this vast expanse.
i wonder about poison. about membranes stretched
thin.
i wonder about fault lines.
i wonder.

and i worry.
about living things
set to
spoil.

25.
"it's time," junior explains.
　　"Henry says: it's time."

　　junior is: rudderless.
　　but.
　　junior is: driven.
　　and i am:
　　carried along.
　　upswept.

　　but still,
　　somehow
　　<always>
　　adrift.

26.
leila grins, beckons with a crooked finger. shines
her *want* outward, beaming.
begins to make her way toward the house.

i follow her, tentative,
fall in line with my family down the winding drive,
my eyes lowered, gaze trained tightly on the ground in
front of me.

my skin feels tight, like steam trapped beneath a
thin layer of cling-wrap.

i am sticky, smothered.
i am a rash,
a fever,
the faint echo of a distant pulse.

i am a hothouse flower,
browned edges wilted, crumbled to a fine powder,
to a dull layer of dust.

my body contracts, pressure builds against my
lungs, along my bones.
mud settles, clots within my veins, weighting me,
cuffing me in rusted shackles. caging me. cutting off my
breath, my circulation, my being.

i am solid.

i am sturdy.
i am heavy as a smooth,
<blank>
slate tombstone.

i am the opposite of antimatter.
i am *now*.

27.

leila looks over her shoulder at me, throws a glance at
shelly.

shelly turns back to me, blinks.

she is thoughtful, brisk, filled with purpose.

"stay here, mel," shelly says with decision. she
shakes her head as though the notion has only just
occurred to her.

"stay here.

we need someone to look out. to listen for sounds."

28.
i pause, considering:
  sounds.

  i nod.

  i will stay here.
  i will look out.
  i will listen.

29.
junior, shelly, and leila slink along, crawl closer. i watch
their figures shrink as they move farther from my sight
line, insects skittering, quivering sensors extended,
crackling with energy. with purpose.

their footsteps cast no echo against the dry
pavement of the pathway, but in the stark silence, in
the vast vortex of the concave canyon, i can just make
out a faint rustling, can just hear the muffled friction of
vines, of winding stalks and bowing stems brushing up
against limbs, then giving way again.

i tense, insides straining against the binding of my
skin, my organs pulsing, my throat constricting. i gasp,
swallow mouthfuls of water, press my tongue against
fistfuls of sand, hard and wet and grainy as cement.
setting.

i am drowning.
still.
again.
always.

30.
i hear:

>   *<static>*
>   *<interference>.*

>   dread traces cold fingers
>   against my throat.

>   i shudder.

>   *<silence.>*
>   *<white noise.>*
>   *<interference.>*

>   then:
>   a click
>   the cock of a trigger
>   the cold, empty clang
>   of metal against
>   metal.

>   i hear
>   the click
>   of a trigger.

>   and
>   i
>   implode.

31.
my stone shield, my cement-set self, bursts open,
shatters, disintegrates.

a wave rushes over me, thick and warm.

the air is charged, magnetic, streaked with fire,
fear, loss.

and i am raw, skinned.

open.

32.
i leak.

    i run.
    i seep.

    i feel myself stumble, stagger, tumble,
    lose my center of gravity.

    i feel the bottom—
    the end of me, my core—
    feel it melt,
    evaporate,
    give way.

    feel myself fall.
    feel *infinity*.

33.
i squeeze my eyes shut,
>   flatten my palms against my ears,
>   press with all of my strength.

>   i try:
>   to stop listening.
>   to shut out the sounds.
>   to quiet the fever.

>   but.
>   it is too late.
>   it is time.

>   it is:
>   *now.*

>   and we are:
>   the message,
>   the moral,
>   the spark.

>   *we.*
>   are:
>   afire.
>   aflame.
>   alight.

we
burn.

we are:
<*helter-skelter*>
chaos.

and
we
are

here.

34.
i breathe:
  in.
  and out.

  the world is back.
  i am back.
  i inhale, sharp and full,
  and just like that—
  <*whoosh*>
  the underneath has settled,
  and i can see colors again.
  dark colors,
  the sorts of shades that
  paint the corners of your consciousness.
  the sorts of shades that
  haunt you.

  they surround me.
  they are all
  around me.

  i breathe.
  i awaken.
  i arise.

  i know why it is that shelly asked me to stay
behind. something to do with rescue, with my *sister*
knowing, even *now*, just what it is i need.

but.
i cannot leave my family. cannot be left behind.
cannot avoid that which i have been chosen for.

i awaken.
i arise.

35.

junior, leila, shelly—they have made their way to the house, just walked right through the front door, sluiced through the atmosphere, passed through this earthly plane like spirits, whispers, wisps.

like suggestions, like shapeless phantasms.

36.
they have left the outer screen door ajar.
    for me.
    they are inviting, inciting. me.
    beckoning me.

37.
i choke.
    i sputter.
    bile rises against
    the back of my throat,
    thick,
    bitter,
    cloying.

    i am drowning.
    still. again.
    always.

38.
but.

    <no.>
    i breathe.

39.
it doesn't take.
　　the world is back.
　　i am back.

　　i clench my jaw, shake my head.
　　swallow the poison back down again.

40.
inside.
    now.

    beyond the flimsy screen door,
    beyond the separation of world and womb.

    i am inside, now,
    standing in the center of the living room
    of the singer's house.

    ‹breathe.›

41.

the man on the sofa shakes his head, pushes himself up on one elbow. sleep crusts the corners of his eyes.

he blinks, shakes his free wrist, peers at his watch. his hair is flattened, pressed against his skull from where he dozed off on the sofa.

he looks small, disoriented. confused.

"what time is it?" he asks. "was i—?"

then he stops. takes in junior:

six feet tall, clad in shadow, cheek spattered, caked with mud.

junior, bearing down on him.

"who are you?" the man on the sofa asks.

he is still uncertain. still not quite concerned, not too terribly worried about the turn that this evening has taken.

he should be.

42.
"Henry has a message for you," junior says.
   "Henry wants you to know:
   you're late.
   you were s'posed to come by weeks ago."

   he smirks.
   "you were s'posed to come hear him. to *listen.*

   "you made a mistake, disrespecting Henry that way.
   but it's all right,
   we can fix this.
   make it right.
   we got a message that you'll hear
   loud and
   clear."

43.
i breathe.
    reel.
    realize:
    this is the blank,
    important man.
    this is *his* house.

    this is where the man who rejected Henry lives.

    that
    —*that*—
    is why we are
    here.

    that is the spark
    that spurred *helter-skelter*.

    <you wouldn't believe the things people waste.>
    <human beings waste all kinds of things.>

    i reel.
    <no ego no i?>
    and the undertow threatens
    to overtake me
    yet again.

44.
junior draws himself farther, higher,
     until he is tall as a tree,
     a tower,
     a tornado.

     he slides his pistol from his waistband,
     cocks it.

     <click.>
     the cold, empty clang
     of metal against metal.

     and i feel
     my *self*
     <no ego no i no before>
     begin to break
     the surface of the water.

45.
click.

i hear a moan: shelly, or possibly the singer,
possibly contemplating what has become of her
now.
the singer, who is bound.
the man on the couch, confused, semiconscious,
still struggling to pierce the eggshell-thin veil
between sleep and wake.
still trying to rise.

my stomach clenches, a swarm of hornets struggle
from deep within, fluttering wings locked in beat.
the ocean swells beneath me.
<breathe.>

46.
the man on the couch seems to realize.
    his eyes dart from junior's face to leila's,
    then to shelly's, and finally, to
    mine.

    i look away.
    paddle furiously, inside my mind's eye.
    try to stay afloat.

    i have been *chosen* for this,
    after all.

    cast away.
    nearly drowned
    swept up
    and into
    the
    current.

    this—
    the *now*—
    helter-skelter—
    this is what it means to be a
    messenger.

    this is what it means
    to spread
    Henry's
    word.

47.
another wave.
    i waver.

    <breathe.>

    i am a cipher.
    i am a whisper.
    i am diaphanous, negative
    space.
    i am the opposite of solid.

    i am antimatter. a black hole.
    a chasm.
    a network of fault lines,
    fractured beyond repair.

    i am a member of this *family*:
    sister, wife,
    daughter.

    i am the undertow, the tide at midnight.
    i am adrift, awash, pulled in every direction.
    choking on swallows of seaweed and salt water.
    floating toward the edges of the horizon.

    i am:
    a message
    a spark,

a groundswell of
trash and
terror.

and
i cannot help this man
any more than i can
quench the fever
dim the fire
douse the flame
that we have—
that my *family* has—
set
to

burn.

48.

the man on the couch purses his lips, tries to contain his fear.

"who are you?" he asks again.

<a threat a promise an unfulfilled premise>
<chaos bloodlust sharp teeth slick canines>
<anger hunger>
<swallow you whole>

i think:
we
are the high tide.

and you
are going
to
drown.

49.
"i'm the devil," junior says.

    "and i'm here to do the devil's business."

50.
then:

    <static>

    then:
    <interference>

    a shriek
    a shudder
    a plea.

    "i don't—"
    the man begins:
    "why—?"

    i am rooted to the ground,
    rotting from the inside.

    bloodstream, brain,
    poisoned.

    i am an outline,
    a suggestion of some former self,
    some long-ago daughter,
    some solid,
    sturdy girl
    who once knew
    how
    to
    swim.

micol ostow

i have been carried to this place,
this *now*,
on a current

treading water
furiously
foolishly.

and i
am

sinking.

●

51.

the man's eyes widen, sharpen, focus on the afterlife as
it bears down.
  "no," he starts, holding out an arm, then changing
course to bury his face
      in the crook of his elbow.

      the singer thrashes, convulses,
      twists and contorts as horror dawns
      with gruesome certainty.

      junior nods. smiles.
      aims the gun.

      "yes,"
      he says.
      "yes."

      he pulls the trigger.

52.
junior pulls the trigger.

    the room ignites.

    i am pulled into a vortex, the relentless, unyielding
pressure of death.

    a meteor shower unfolds, angry chunks of blazing,
boiling rock, raining nuclear fire,

    rocketing through the atmosphere and crushing
down.

    singeing us, scorching us, flaying the flesh from our
charred, stripped-down bones.

    burying us alive.

53.
sounds.

they are inescapable.
they come to me, unbidden.

a gunshot, clapping like a sonic boom.
a muffled cry through the oily cloth of the
singer's gag.
the deep, desperate drowning of the man on the
couch as blood seeps down his shirtfront.
leila's laughter.

from somewhere deep, someplace far, buried
within the fault lines of the house,
a scream, a shriek, pierces the air, punctuates the
explosion, the bottomless blast, the burst of death,
blood
<chaos>.

it howls,
stirs,
strains
formlessly,
wordlessly,
against the
spark
that junior has
ignited.

it takes a beat,
a breath,
a split-second,
razor's-edge moment
before i realize:

the sound
the shriek

the scream

the unfathomable,
infinite
terror

is
mine.

54.

<breathe.>

i wait.
i waver.

i collect myself again,
curl inward.
glance toward shelly,
toward my *sister*.

her eyes are a vacant mask.
but her lips—
her lips—
are upturned.

and she does not meet my gaze.

i wait.
i waver.
i collect myself again.
curl inward.
fight against the
thick, sour tangle
of seaweed,
sand
of sunken spoils
rising,
crawling,

clawing their way up my throat
drowning me
choking me
off.

55.
i want to go away
    again.

    want to
    <*breathe*>
    and be less than
    nothing,
    a trace element of
    a long-ago landmass.

    i want to be empty.
    to be absence.
    to be a yawning, gaping
    vortex.

    i want to be the evening
    tide.

    <*impossible*>
    <*no ego no i no before*>
    <*nothing that never ends*>

    i want to be carried out
    by the
    undertow.

56.
the smoky stench of gunpowder,
    the blooms of life that spread beneath the man on
the couch,
    the sound of aftermath,
    of half-life, of
    <love and>
    terror—
    they ring, vibrate,
    radiate.

    the shrieks, the screams, the splintering cries, they
    envelop me.
    clutch me.
    cloak me
    like a hangman's hood.

    leila laughs.
    shelly grins.
    and junior cocks the trigger on his pistol once
again.

    i swoon.

57.
shelly gestures to junior,
    whispers a secret code,
    somehow persuades him to set aside the gun
    for now.

    she steps beside me, places a firm hand on the
narrow curve at the small of my back.
    steadies me. turns her grin in my direction, as a
loved one would.

    she knows, of course.
    my sister.
    knows. just what i need.

    <*breathe.*>

    her eyes are round.
    open.

    i reel.
    i realize:

    she glows.
    she *shines*.
    joyful tears trace footpaths
    down her cheeks,

a baptism
amidst a bloodbath.

she runs a pink tongue along the fragile skin of her
upper lip
<*first the dogs eat the dogs eat first*>,
hungry.

58.
she leans forward, reaches out a steady arm. pokes at
the man on the couch
   <—*the* dying *man; that is what he is, right now,*
dying—>
   so that his body shifts.

   i buckle.

   she pulls her hand back, considers it. takes in the
bright patch of blood—rich, rust colored, and thick—
now tattooed into the fat, fleshy point of her fingertip.
licks her lips again.

   i sway.
   <*breathe.*>

   she grabs at my wrist. i feel the sticky underside of
her finger, know that when we pull apart, she will have
left a smudgy red imprint in her wake.
   <*breathe.*>

   "let's go," she says, eyebrows aloft. she juts her chin
toward junior, toward his dangling gun. raises her knife,
gleaming deadly, her meaning starkly clear.

   "let's go.
   we still have to do the other one."

59.
shelly turns to leila, who smiles.
  behind her darting, downcast eyes,
  leila smiles.

  leila knows, has always known,
  how best to make a person bleed.

  leila is a coil,
  a live wire,
  a potent cache of
  wicked intent.

  leila is love
  and terror.

  whereas shelly is
  —suddenly—
  chaos.

  shelly is
  charged
  and churning.
  she is a black hole,
  a bottomless pit.

  she is sinister,
  she is danger.
  she is *so much.*

shelly.
is.

all of her fractures—
her fault lines—
they have split.

her damage—
her past-life—
it collapses,
rushes through the
open spaces of her
pores.

leila is quiet cunning.
junior is a dark foot soldier.

but shelly is
damage.

her eyes dance,
her skin thrums,
the corners of her mouth
twitch.

the
<dying>
man's blood stains her face,

her forehead,
her cheeks
so that she is alive,
even *more*
than before.

so that she blossoms from his pain,
feeds from it,

as she scurries
back and forth
through the shrieking space,
testing knots,
turning chairs and tables over,
frenzied.

clearing a space
for death,
for darkness,
for pain.

for the call of
helter-skelter.

she is
<*so much*>
more.
alive.

but.
she is not
my sister.

not
now.

not
anymore.

60.
shelly is impatient.

    she wants to fill her hollow spaces in sharp, swift
order.

    wants to spread Henry's word. wants to make
dangerous music.

    she writhes and wriggles, alive with the anticipation.
    her knife waves.

"let's go," she repeats, her voice more urgent, more
insistent, this time.

    "let's go. there's still another one.
    we still have to do the other one.
    junior saved her for us."

the other one.
the singer.
<junior saved her for us.>

a life-size barbie,
a living doll.
a whole and perfect creature.

shuddering in the corner of the living room,
shivering in her thin nightgown.
pleading with us, *at* us—
pleading with her swollen, sea-glass eyes.

doomed.

61.
shelly stops, tips her head back, listens for sounds.
　　the air outside—
　　the air *beyond*—
　　is calm, quiet,
　　smooth as the surface of a lake,

　　betraying none of the chaos of our
　　mission.

　　she regards me, shelly,
　　seems to
　　<know>
　　understand
　　how i suddenly
　　waver.

　　but.
　　i have quieted,
　　finally,
　　for *now*—

　　swallowed the echoes of my
　　bottomless scream.
　　for *now*.

　　this seems to satisfy her.
　　my *sister*.

"let's go," she says.
"let's spread the message.
the word.
the terror.
for Henry."

before

when i was six years old,
    i drowned.

    since then, there has only been *always:*
    fault lines, fragments,
    well-deep tide pools.

    a pull, guiding me.
    pushing, stretching.
    applying pressure in every direction
    but home.

    since then, there has been only
    the undertow.

    at night, i dream.
    at night, the afterlife washes over me,
    stiff and bright.
    probing.

    i know it is the afterlife—
    not me, *not* i, *and certainly not, never* now—
    i know that it is merely some formless half-life,
    a premise,
    a promise
    of a *maybe-infinity.*

micol ostow

i know this
from the slow, measured sound,
the metered mantra of mirror-mel:

<breathe.>

mirror-mel has tips, tricks,
techniques.
she knows special secrets,
ways of squirming out,
of disentangling,
of secreting herself
away.

she has methods of extricating herself from
thick, heavy hands.
<breathe.>

she tucks herself up,
folds herself inward,
collapses in on herself.

she slides easily out from under crushing warmth,
from smothering, suffocating weight.
from beneath. from the underneath.

mirror-mel has never known the smell of whiskey.
mirror-mel has no uncle jack, nor any
blank, empty mother.

family

but.

mirror-mel is not me.
she is the opposite of me.
she is an outline,
a suggestion of my shape.

and at night,
when uncle jack comes,
i am alone.

when i was six years old, i drowned.

i *was* drowned. i was
< *held down filled up choked off* >
covered, stifled, smothered.

it was the first time.
it was:
< *uncles and elbows* >
< *knees pinned apart* >
< *love and* >
terror,
sharp and bright.

it was:
whiskey breath,
roaming hands.

it was:
waves. swells. tidal shifts.
swift.
imperceptible.
but unmistakable.

it was:
infinity.
a moment without beginning or
end.
a moment of bloodlust.
of chaos.
a moment that swallowed me
whole.

when i was six years old,
i drowned.
for the first time.

was drowned.
for the first time.

when i was six years old, uncle jack sealed his
mouth against my own.
he gasped, flailed against me, struggled to
resuscitate himself,
to breathe life back into his own eternity,
his own *infinity.*

he split me open,
pressed himself into every hollow place,
pushed against me
so that there wasn't room for me
<no ego no i no why>,
no space, no safety
inside of my own
skin.

i couldn't speak,
couldn't scream.
couldn't swallow or
breathe.

couldn't do anything but
drift.
but
dream.

awake,
i dreamed.

of:
oceans,
tidal waves,
tsunamis.

of:
chaos.

of:
abandoned cargo,
of sunken, rusted
treasure,
weighted down,
soaked and
solid,
rotting beneath the
surface.

of:
valueless artifacts,
set to spoil
beneath,
in the underneath.

when i was six years old, i thrashed against
heaping mouthfuls of stinging salt water.

i did my best to hold my breath,
to stave off the looming *infinite*,
the *ever-after*.

i did my best to stay
tightly bound,

to stay
together,
alone.

and when i heard my mother
poised atop the staircase,

heard my mother

<breathe:
in.
out.>

know.

know, but un-know.
hear, but not-hear.

when i heard my mother
choose the either/or,

heard my mother
offer me up as a
<sacrifice>,
heard her
decide to let me
drown—

that was
<yes oh yes>
the precise moment—

the heartbeat,

the hair's breath—

the
<*blink*>,
when i

shattered.

i fractured.
i shrank.

that was the split second
when i collapsed inward on myself,
spiraled off into my own
orbit.

blurred the edges of my own existence.

that was when i left my hollowed-out husk,
set off in search of the edge of the horizon.
embraced the chaos of *infinity*.
surrendered to the
undertow.

when i was six years old, i drowned.

but i have always been broken.

now

<breathe.>

    my hands are streaked with blood that is not my own.
    my hands are streaked with blood, and there is screaming.

    somewhere in the house, there is a high-pitched, constant screaming that has, by now, dissolved into the sort of ambient white noise that a person could tune out, easily enough, if she were so inclined. canned horror, like you might find on a sound-effects recording, or at a theme-park haunted house.

    voices. bodies. and panic.
    so much panic.

    i tune the shrieking, high-pitched panic, the shrill vibrato out, send it to a separate frequency, set it aside for the immediate future, as i tend to the issue of my stained, shaking hands.
    how did they get this way?
    i know the answer. i don't want to know the answer, but these are things i can't undo, can't un-know.
    <helter–skelter.>

my hands shake, the blood pooling into the
crevices of my gnawed-down cuticles.

even now, amidst the chaos, i am struck by how
i have my mother's hands, though hers have never
looked like this. would never look like this.

how strange to think that i should have my
mother's hands. since i no longer have my mother, a
mother,
    any mother.

how strange to think of what has become of me, of
my half-life,
    even of mirror-mel.

how unexpected to find one's fault lines etched
deep;
    set in stone,
    permanent.

how unexpected to discover that
the mirror-image remains
even after the curtain,
the veil,
the hazy woolen netting
has been
drawn.

how strange to think of what i've known—

of what i've come to know—
as *family*.

Henry says:
everything belongs to everyone.

Henry says:
there is no *i*. no *ego*.
no need for
parents.

but.

i did, i think.
i needed.
<things could have been so different. >

i needed a mother.
needed more than just an outline,
more than the mere suggestion
of her self.

needed so many things
to fill myself
up.

Henry saw that.
He sees. everything.

and with my need
He makes Himself
whole.

Henry says:
there is only *family*.
our family.

Henry is
<*love*
and terror>
infinity.

Henry says there is no
belonging,
no *i*,

but:
Henry has us—
all the matchstick thin,
flimsy
paper-doll tracings—
all of the delicate, drowned
outlines—

all the members of our
family
to do

His
bidding.

Henry is the one who found the
<*sacrifice*>
singer
and the blank, important
<*dying*>
man.

the singer struggles.
shelly has corralled her, wrestled her into the
center of the living room, where she, leila, and junior
have trussed the broken, battered china doll in twine.
bound, the singer surveys the scene, the carnage,
the chaos. she passes flickering, fluttering pupils over
the ruined man on the couch.
eyes wide with disbelief, round with dawning
realization, she struggles.
she strains, breaks, thrashes against the current,
digs her heels into the *now*. she heaves, hiccups, twists
with pain, bright and swift.
she bleeds.

i listen for sounds.

crouched in the corner,
flattened against the sturdy stucco wall, i

<breathe>
focus.

i listen for sounds.

they come to me, unbidden.
choked, thick, drenched with helplessness,
they come to me.
unbidden.

the singer pleads, cries, begs.
she knows nothing of her husband's broken
promise,
nothing of our fractured family's gravitational pull.
our orbit.

she *wants*.
wants
life.

she moans. the sound is soft, but still unmistakable
amidst the deafening mayhem.
it rises above the screaming, gaping, oozing chaos.
i hear her. shelly hears her.
there is no way to not-hear her.

she seeps.
from somewhere deep, someplace inescapable, she

spills across the floorboards of her violated compound.
she dissolves.

    she is ephemeral. diaphanous.

    she is, suddenly, *everything*.

    i shudder, stagger, heave.
    i shut my eyes, open them again.

    i take in shelly.
    she hovers, poised above the singer, this
    suggestion of a fantasy
    who is little more
    than a
    husk of herself, really.
    little more
    than the remains of her own
    half-life.

    the singer is emptying out. hollowing.
    maybe shelly is, too.
    maybe. i think.
    maybe we all are.
    maybe this is our *now*, the *now* that we have finally
come to,
    collectively, pedaling furiously, foolishly.
    paddling directly into the eye of the
    storm.

shelly pauses, wipes the back of her palm against
her forehead, leaves behind a streak of rust-colored
blood, stark against the blank expanse of her pale skin.

she is marked.
she is endless.
she is forever.
she is *now.*

and she is not my sister
anymore.

my hands are streaked with blood that is not my
own.
my hands are streaked with blood that is not my
own, and the horror-movie sound effects persist.

⟨. . .⟩
interference
white noise.
torrents of skin and bone.
skin and bone, and blood.
so much blood.

rushes, tidal waves, well-deep reflecting pools of
blood, raging everywhere,
catching in every corner, flickering and taking hold
like a thick, coppery fever.

leila does as Henry commanded: she scrawls
symbols, secrets,
horror-story hieroglyphics all along the wall:

RISE
PIG
DEATH
HELTER-SKELTER.

she writes in blood
and laughs to see
the words form at her
hands.

part IV

end

junior holds the singer down.
     shelly's arm rises, the glint of her knife's blade
throwing a spark that arcs,
         that glimmers, that gleams like a supernova
         burning through the atmosphere.

     sounds come to me, unbidden.
     it takes a long time for a person to let go.
     sometimes.

     i shudder.
     i swoon.
     i stagger.

     this,
     i realize—

     it is my *either/or*,
     my *half-life*,
     my *underneath*.

     this moment is my witching hour,
     my midnight tide.

     i burn.

i melt.
i sink.
i drown.

bodies. there are bodies everywhere.
and the bodies are broken.

we are *all* broken.
we are all supernovas.
black holes, disintegrating.

we are all:
crushing, pulling, recoiling,
unraveling.

we are all:
collapsing in on ourselves, like dying stars.

shelly calls to me.

i look up from where i cower, crouched,
to see her holding out her knife.

it is a suggestion, the knife.
it is:
an urging.
an invitation to join
my *family.*

the knife is a call to

awaken,
to embrace
—to *embody*—
the chaos.

it is a sound to spread the
message.
to *be* the message.
to be the love
<and terror>.

the knife is a suggestion to step forward and out of
my hollow husk,
to emerge beyond the outline of my own shadow
tracing.

to be solid.
to be *self.*
to become.

i reel.

i realize:
i have been left behind.
i have been broken.
i have.
always.

but.

this—
this is my orbit,
my spiral.
my own *infinity*.
my own
now.

and *now*
i can
awaken.
arise.

i *can*.

i have—
always—
contracted, recoiled,
refracted.

have always,
always,
wanted to patch the fault lines of my
cracked, jagged surfaces.

i have always wanted to staunch the waves of fever,
the rushes of heat.

infinity has always felt impossible to me.

there is nothing, after all, that doesn't
end.

i have always been alone,
have always felt empty.
always.
still.

but.

still,
i have *now*.
i am *now*.

and
now:

i rise.

breathe:
in.
and out.

now:
i am solid.
i am sturdy.
i am heavy as a smooth slate tombstone.
i am the opposite of antimatter.

i *am*.
now.

shelly calls to me.
leila cackles.
junior drips with *want*.
the undertow beckons.
sounds come to me,
unbidden.

<come to now.>

and *now:*
i know.
finally.

finally,
i know:

i am *not*:
sister,
wife,
daughter.

not ephemeral.
not a paper doll.

i have no mother.

micol ostow

never had a father.

<i can be your everything.>

i am:
empty,
bottomless,
rudderless.

still.
yet.
yes.

i breathe:

in.
and out.
in.
and out.

and then:

i rise.

<yes.>

finally,
endlessly

—*always*—
at last:

my half-life rushes over me, fevered and thick.
i inhale, swallow deeply.

take in the washed colors of the
afterlife.

i see them:

the edges of the horizon, the mouth of the chasm.
the seams of my fractured body's fault lines.

i see them so clearly
<*yes oh yes*>,
see the outline of each
as though each is a looming midnight
tidal wave.

there has never been a time that i was not
drowning.

<*never*>
<*always*>
<*infinity*>.

there has never been a time that i was not
adrift,

afloat,

pulled by an
invisible membrane.
an undertow.

there has never been a time that i was not haunted,
shadowed by a mirror-self,
cement-set
deep within my own
rotting half-life.

there has never been a time that i was not
set to spoil.

but.
still.
now:

my fault lines,
my fissures, my rivulets—
the scar tissue tracings that
seal up my fractured spaces—
they can entwine.
can bind.

can choke me,
cut me off,
tie me down.

they can.

or.
they could—
they *can*—
be a lifeline.

now.

there has never been a time that wasn't
now.

i know this, now.
now, i know.

there has never been a part of me
that existed only as a
photo negative.
only as a reflection.
only as an *either/or.*

there is no such thing as mirror-mel.
no half-life version of my being.

there is only
my *self,*
here.
now.

alone.
damaged.
bruised.
fault lines, fissures,
scar-tissue tracings.
fractured, yes
<yes oh yes>,

but solid, sturdy, smooth as a slate tombstone.

lit from the inside
like a sliver of moonstone.

adrift,
but still
afloat.

still.
here.

now.

this is my *self.*
this is my *now.*

and so:
i blink.

i breathe:

in.
and out.

i reel.
i rise.

i glance at the rimless reflecting pools of
shelly's dead-eyed gaze,
another not-mother, not-sister,
not-self, swirling in her own
whirlpool;
drowned, delirious.

she is *not* my shadow-self,
but rather,
a darkened cloud of potent, poisoned
chaos.
she *is.*

and
i
can be
the
light.

i *can.*

there is
<*there* is>

micol ostow

a
lifeline.

a way to fight the tide.
a sliver of moonstone, lit from the
inside.

even here.
even *now*.

there is a foothold,
a path carved
deep within the cracks and crags
<*fault lines*>
of the desert canyons.

and it is—
it can be—
mine.

Henry says:
there is no *before*.
just *now*.
an always, ever-spinning,
infinite
now.

but.

now:
alone,
without the premise,
the promise of
a *family*,
i am: adrift.
but still: afloat.

i know that,
now.
now,
i know.

so:
in the *now*—
from deep within the tide pools of
my own,
my *only*
now—

i lunge forward, swift and sure.
snatch the knife from shelly's clenched fist.
swallow against the glee
that spreads the corners of her mouth
from cheek to cheek.

in a frenzied,
fevered
burst,

i charge.
i swipe.

i slice
at the singer's
binding.

i set her
free.

a blink.
a beat.
a hiccup.

the room turns over,
rolls inside out,
tilted by the power of my sudden
current,
swift and sure.

in a dazzle of stardust, the singer is
gone;
out the door and into the inky night,

streaking like a meteor.
she is a whisper, a wisp.
a cipher.

released from the riptide.

saved.

it is almost as though
she never even
existed to begin with.

i breathe:
in.
and out.

i listen for sounds:

the rhythm of my heartbeat
keeping time
against
the pulsing
of the
undertow.

i breathe.
i listen for sounds.
i come to *now*.
back to *now*.

always,
infinitely
now.

i was a messenger.

i had a *family*.
but
this—
this is my
now.
and i am not
sorry.

the streams of worry
of fear
have begun to ebb
even beneath the constant pounding of
Henry's pills.

even beneath
the raging tide
i have a moment
of well-deep
stillness.

and when junior starts—
when he steps
forward,
looming like a twister,
like an all-consuming
typhoon—

when he moves
toward me,

i turn.
feint forward,
uproot myself.
skirt him nimbly,
shift so swiftly,
so imperceptibly,

that in a
beat,
a blink,
a pulse,

within a momentary,
coiled pause:
i find
a rushing
current.
a wave.

slippery
but still
a foothold.

still a cloud-shape that will
guide me
toward the
horizon.

when i was six years old, i drowned.

<luckily, it didn't take.>

and *now*:

i *swim.*

my undertow tugs
like an invisible membrane,
guiding me to a lifeline,
toward a rushing stream,
a current,
a fresh, clean channel
that beckons
just beyond the boundaries
of the flimsy screen door.

i will mark a path of moonstone, i know.
i *know.*

the singer is—
was—
stardust,
a whisper,
a wisp,
a cipher,
a ghost.

while i am merely
a

shipwreck.

sunken.

but

tides are guided
by the gleam of the moon.
and so am
i.

mirror-mel would say that
fractures,
fault lines—
that they follow you.
that *broken* is
forever.
infinite.
that shadows can't be
shed.
mirror-mel would say that
magic
is only a
mirage.

but.
there is no such thing as *either/or.*
no such thing as mirror-mel.
no half-life

and never—
not ever—
before.

there is only my
self.
here.
now.
rusted,
but still reaching,
guided by the gleam
of the moon.

so in the *now*
i tear, fevered,
out the front door of this house,
charging past this moment,
streaking like a
supernova,
lighting up the atmosphere,

glittering
burning
throwing sparks.

the road beyond the canyon stretches far,
yawning black and open,
marked by scattered glints of moonstone.
a cluster.

a constellation.
a galaxy.
that is
mine.

this is the *now*.
my now.

this—
this is my *after*.
it *is*.

my *before*.
my *always*,

i am:
broken.
but i am:
solid.

i am:
afloat
but i ride the pressing, churning current.
the tide.

i
swim.

i am a shipwreck,

sunken treasure,
lit by moonstone.
rotted,
rusted,
alight, aflight,
afire.

but:
i *have*
chosen.

i *have.*

this
now;

it is
mine.
it is only
my
own.
and as i
<streak/stream/shine>
flee the tangled webbing of my
tainted,
tattered,
fragile
family—

f
a
m
i
l
y

i *know.*
finally.

finally,
i know:

that there is
no such thing as
infinity,
after all.

that there is
nothing—
nothing—
after all,

that doesn't

end.

acknowledgments

This book was a leap of faith for me in many ways, and would certainly never have come to be without the love, guidance, and support of many people.

My most sincere gratitude goes to my agent, Jodi Reamer of Writers House, who has helped to shape the evolution of my writing career, and who managed to keep an open mind when I asked if she'd like to see a verse novel about the Manson Family. Thanks also to her trusty right hand, Alec Shane.

My peers and advisors at Vermont College of Fine Arts were endlessly generous with their time, insight, and warmth, without which I might never have moved out of my creative comfort zone. In particular, Tim Wynne-Jones quite literally (and quite forcefully) insisted that I try my hand at something new, and Rita Williams Garcia offered invaluable feedback on early pages. Gwenda Bond, Gene Brenek, and Shawn Stout—there's no one I'd rather storm Noble with than the three of you.

Elizabeth Law at Egmont USA is responsible for all of the very best parts of this book. Her early enthusiasm for the manuscript was matched only by the caliber of her editorial direction. I can't imagine what *family* would have been without her insight.

Bottomless appreciation goes also to the entire extended Egmont crew: Mary Albi, Katie Halata, Alison Weiss, Becky Green, Doug Pocock, and Gordon

Vanderkamp. Nico Medina, you understood my book intrinsically.

Hugs, kisses, and buckets of good karma to Katharine Sise and Nova Ren Suma, my early readers and always-muses. I am in awe of the both of you.

And finally, I am blessed with a wide network of family of my own, all of whom mean everything to me. My in-laws Len, Fleur, Liz, and Josh Harlan have welcomed me into the fold unconditionally. My brother, David Ostow, inspires, challenges, and amuses me. My mother, Carmen Ostow, schooled me in Stephen King and slasher movies, and my father, Jerry Ostow, tolerated (and sometimes even supported) our obsession with the macabre.

As for my husband, Noah Harlan—you are proof-positive of the existence of miracles. I love you.

Thank you, thank you, thank you.